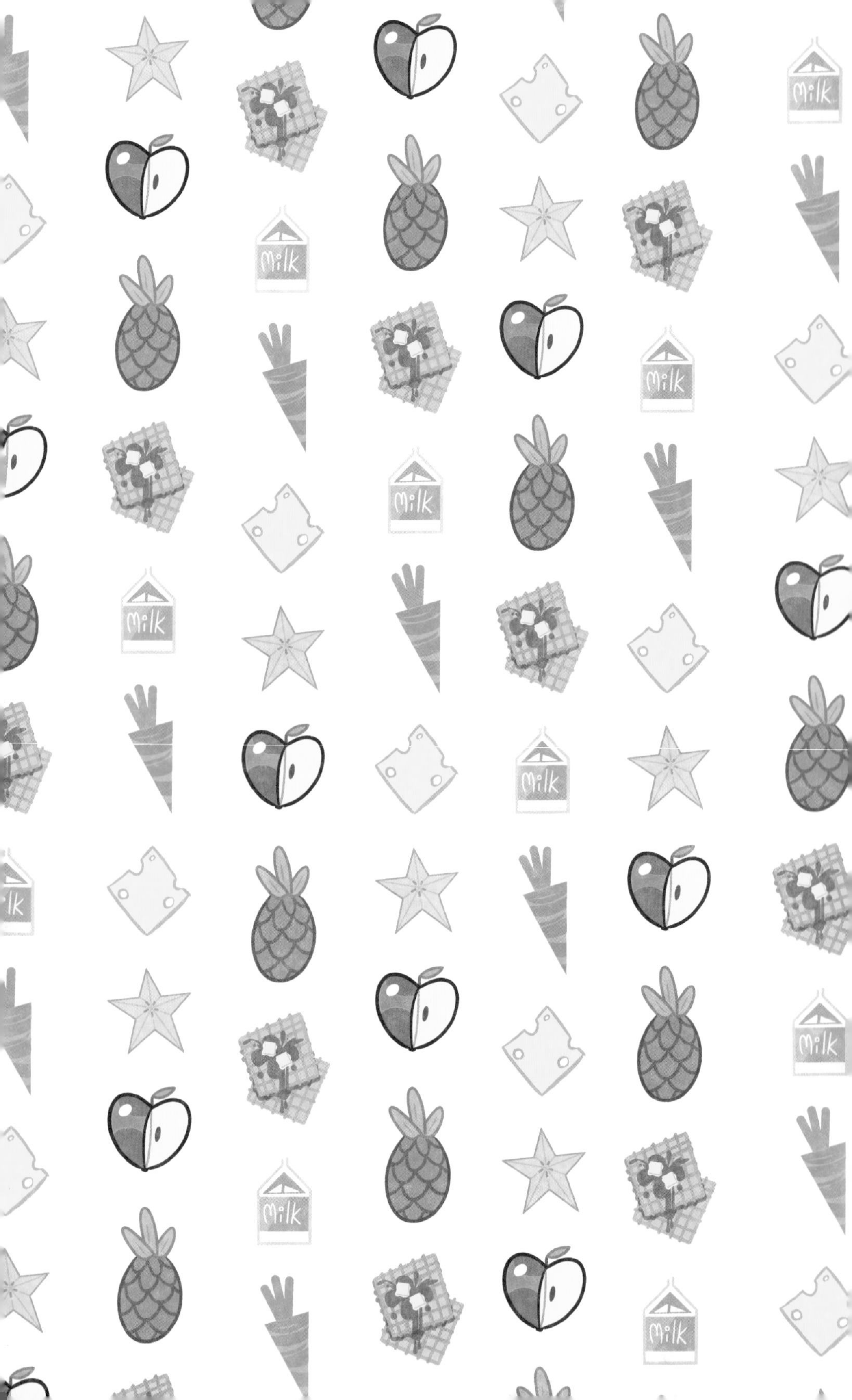
Milk

POWER LUNCH

FIRST COURSE

by
J. Torres & Dean Trippe

lettered by
Ed Brisson

designed by
Keith Wood

edited by
James Lucas Jones

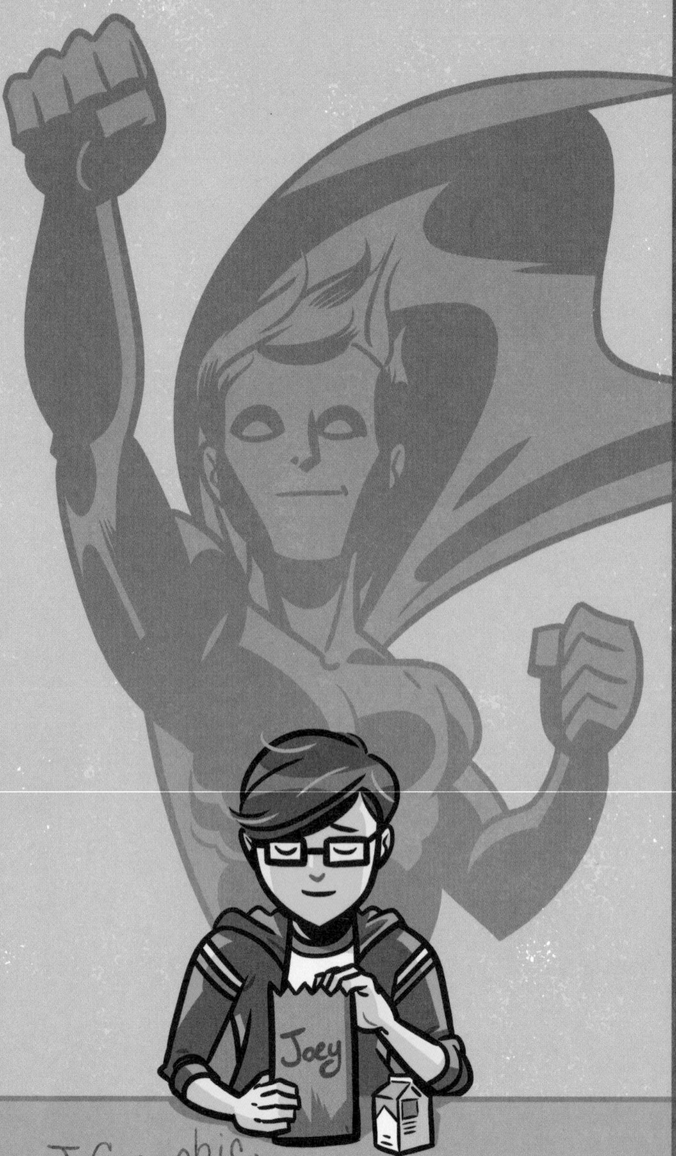
Joey

Published by
Oni Press, Inc.

publisher
Joe Nozemack

editor in chief
James Lucas Jones

operations director
George Rohac

art director
Keith Wood

marketing director
Cory Casoni

editor
Jill Beaton

editor
Charlie Chu

production assistant
Douglas E. Sherwood

Oni Press, Inc.
1305 SE M.L.K. Jr. Blvd.
Suite A
Portland, OR 97214
USA

onipress.com
jtorresonline.com
deantrippe.com

First edition: October 2011

ISBN 978-1-934964-70-5

Library of Congress Control Number: 2011927649

10 9 8 7 6 5 4 3 2 1

Printed by TWP America, Inc. in Singapore, Singapore.

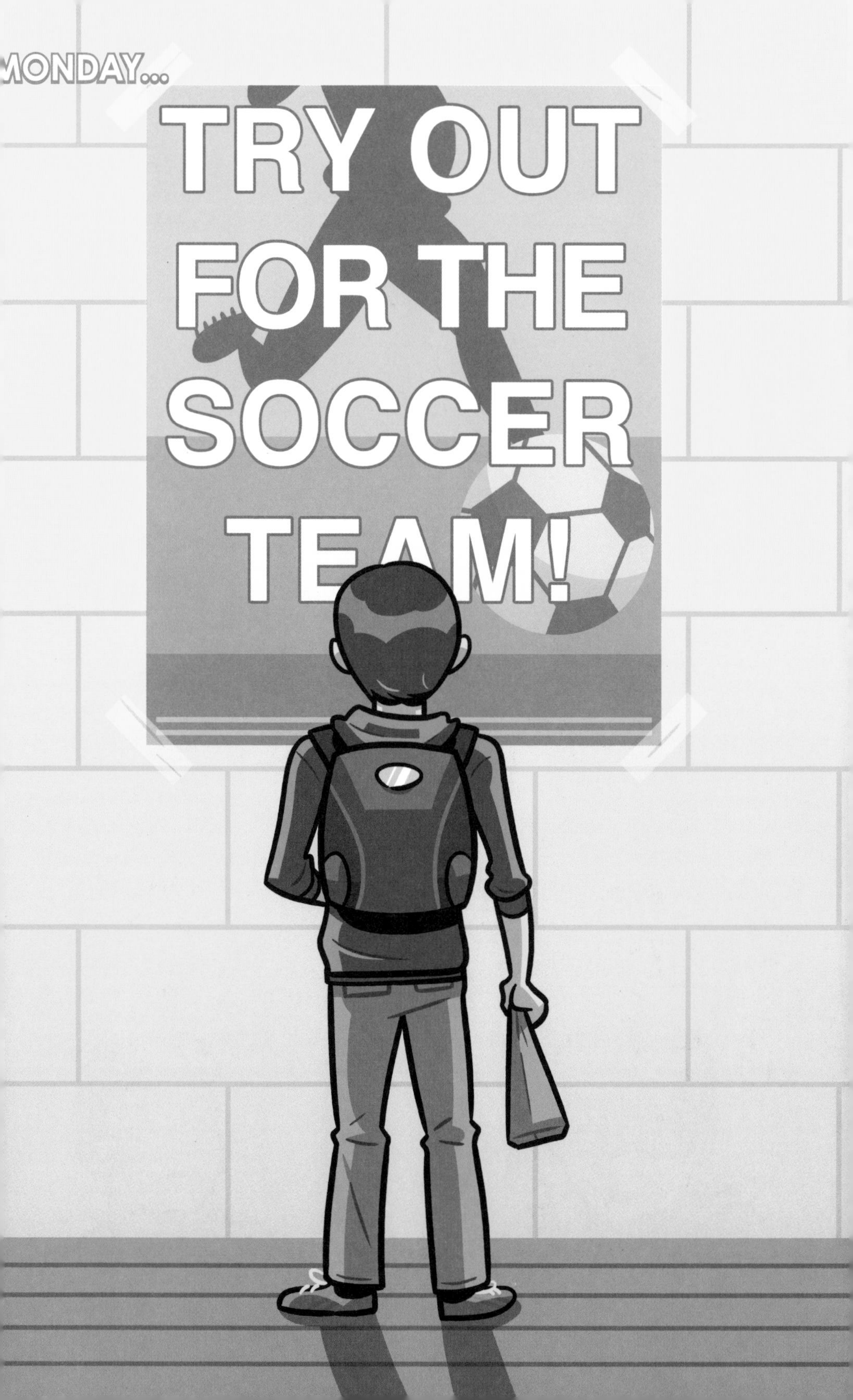
MONDAY...
TRY OUT FOR THE SOCCER TEAM!

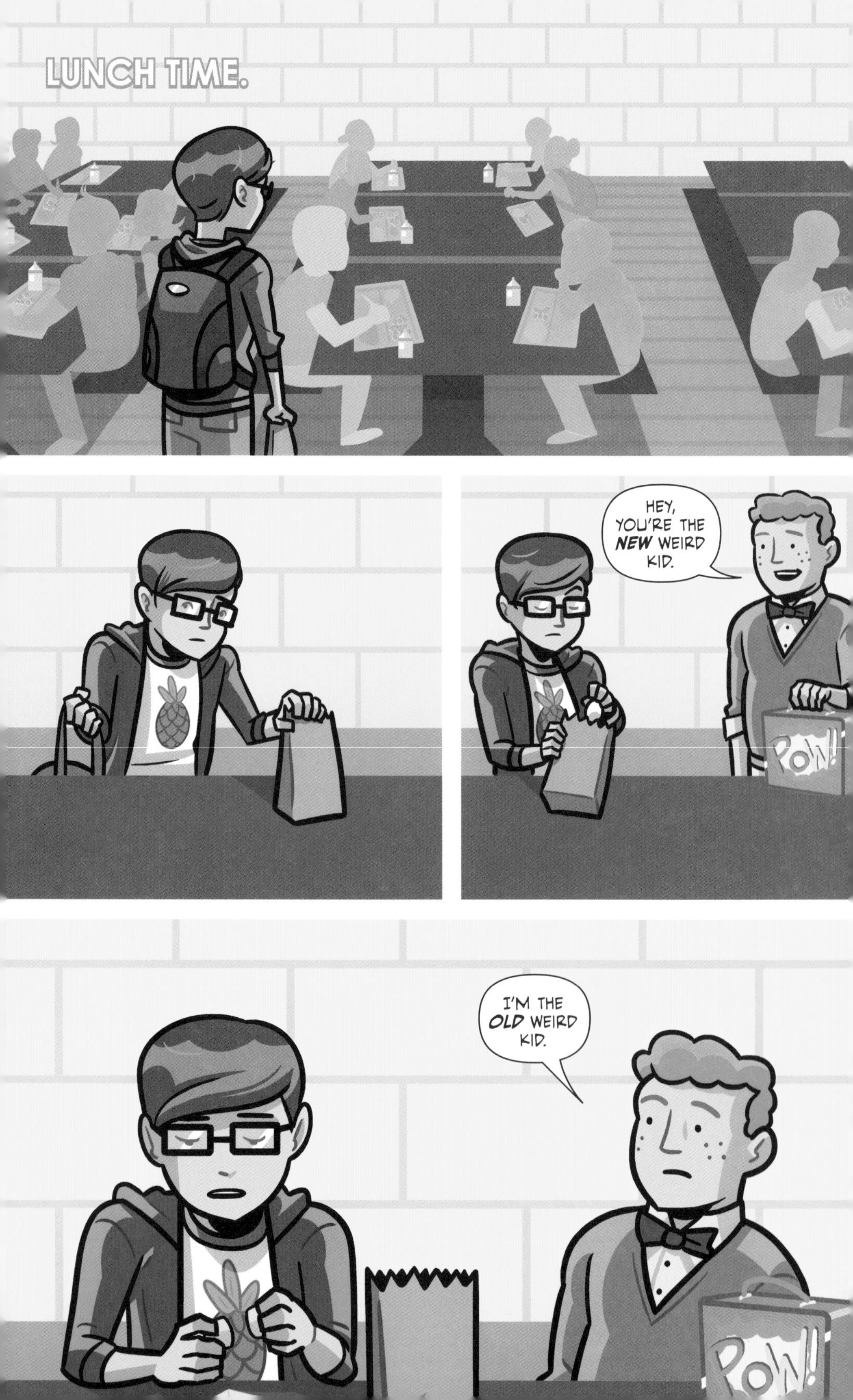
LUNCH TIME.
HEY, YOU'RE THE *NEW* WEIRD KID.
POW!
I'M THE *OLD* WEIRD KID.
POW!

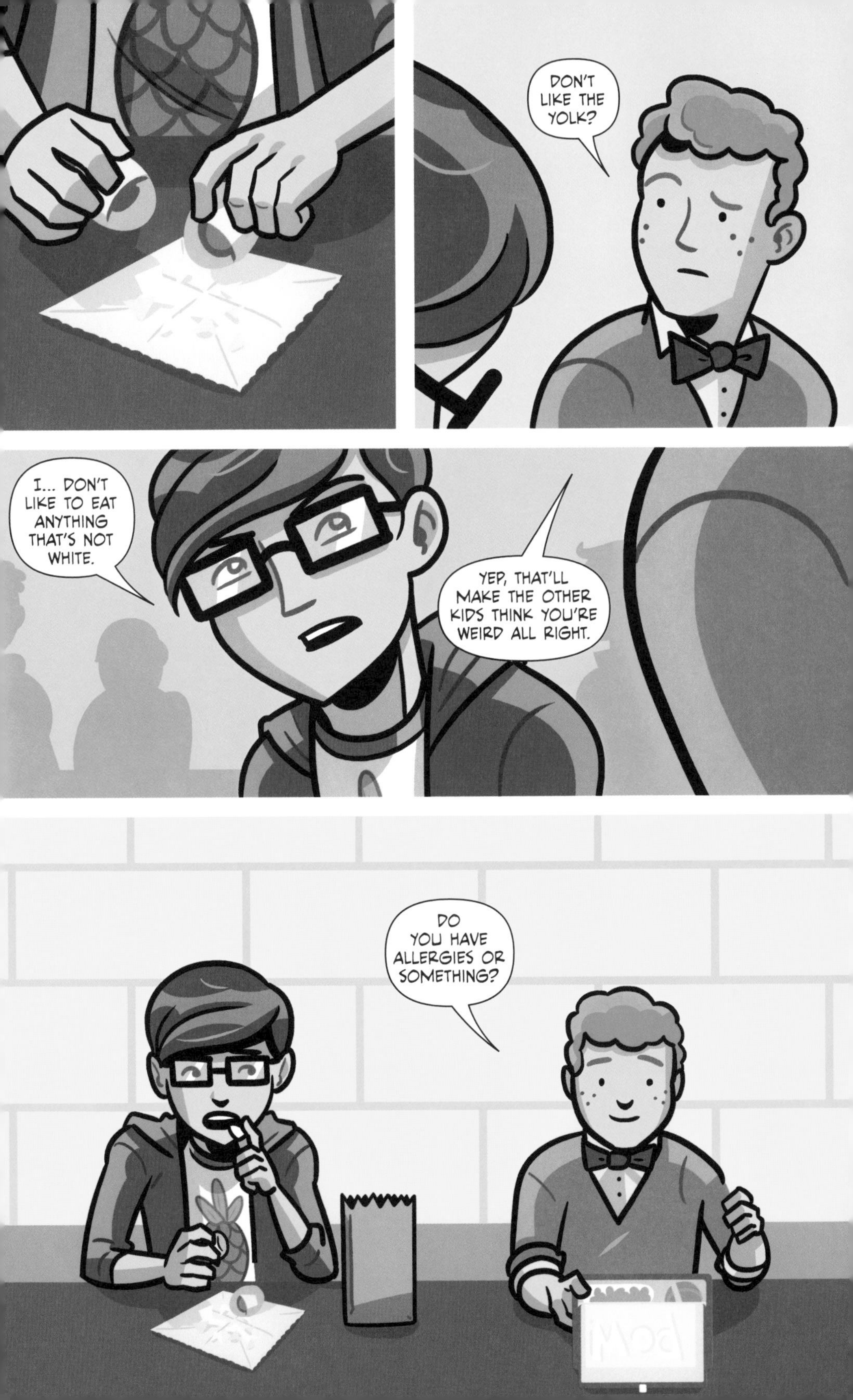
DON'T LIKE THE YOLK?
I... DON'T LIKE TO EAT ANYTHING THAT'S NOT WHITE.
YEP, THAT'LL MAKE THE OTHER KIDS THINK YOU'RE WEIRD ALL RIGHT.
DO YOU HAVE ALLERGIES OR SOMETHING?

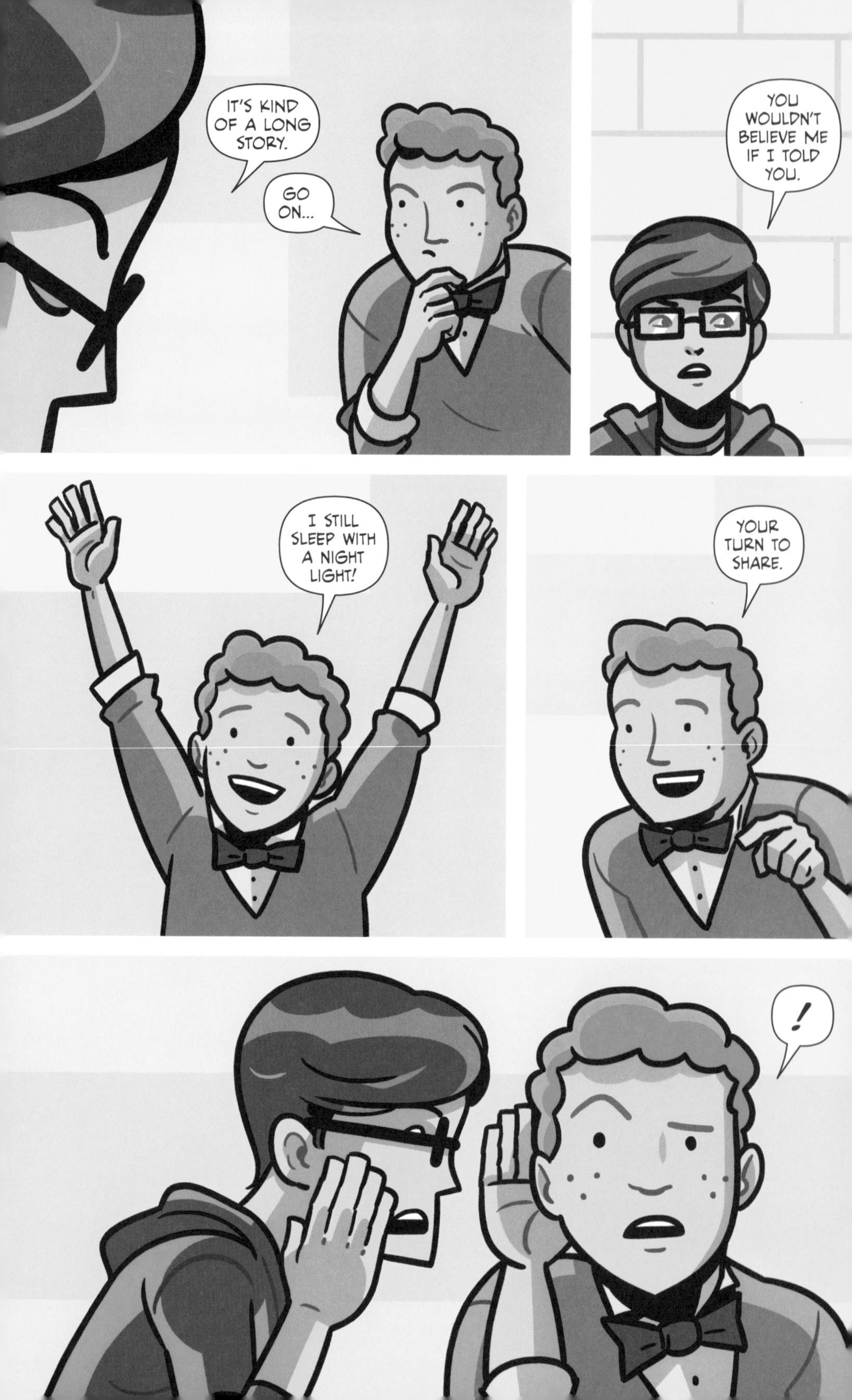
IT'S KIND OF A LONG STORY.
GO ON...
YOU WOULDN'T BELIEVE ME IF I TOLD YOU.
I STILL SLEEP WITH A NIGHT LIGHT!
YOUR TURN TO SHARE.
!

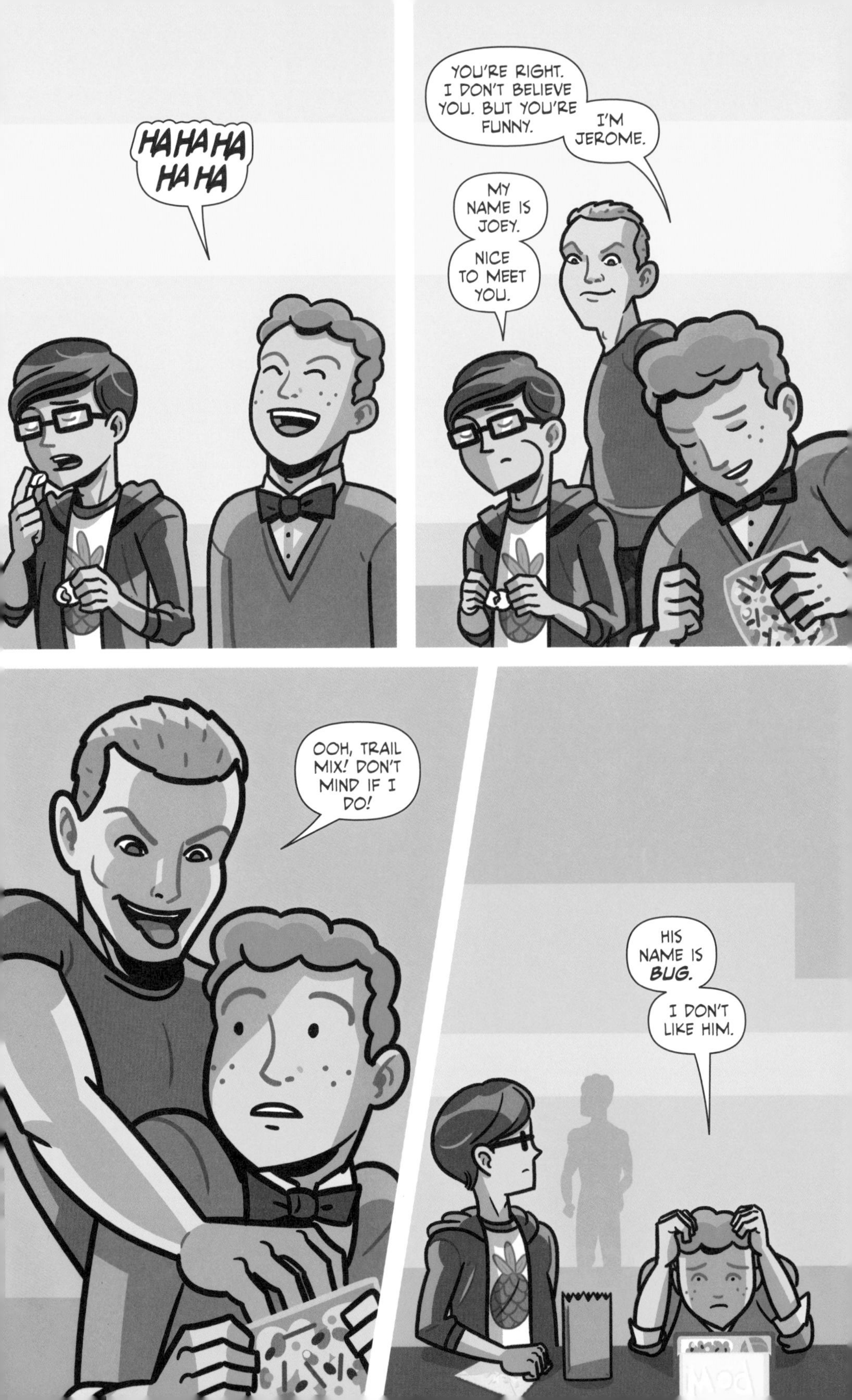
HAHAHA HAHA
YOU'RE RIGHT. I DON'T BELIEVE YOU. BUT YOU'RE FUNNY.
I'M JEROME.
MY NAME IS JOEY.
NICE TO MEET YOU.
OOH, TRAIL MIX! DON'T MIND IF I DO!
HIS NAME IS BUG.
I DON'T LIKE HIM.

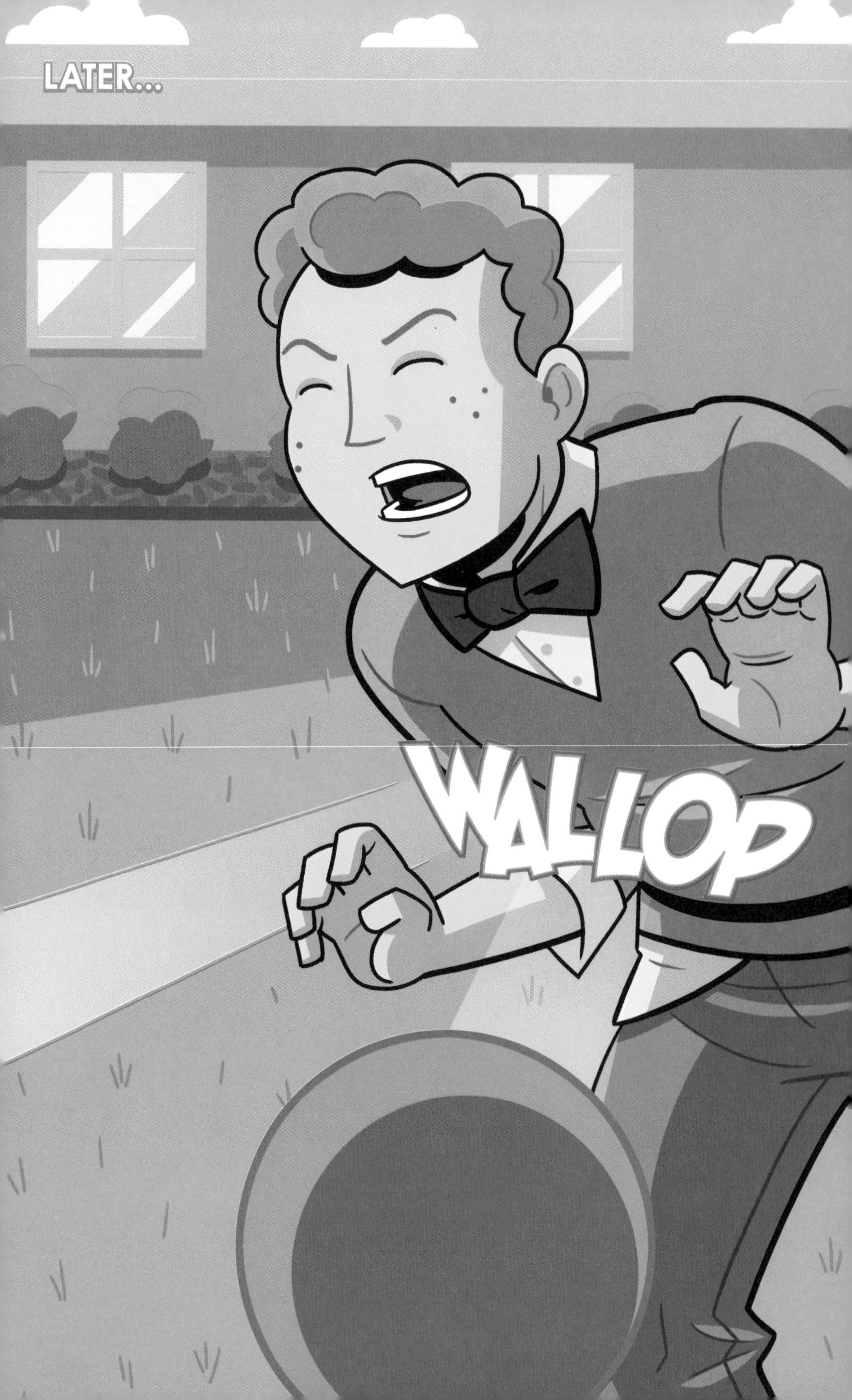
LATER...
WALLOP

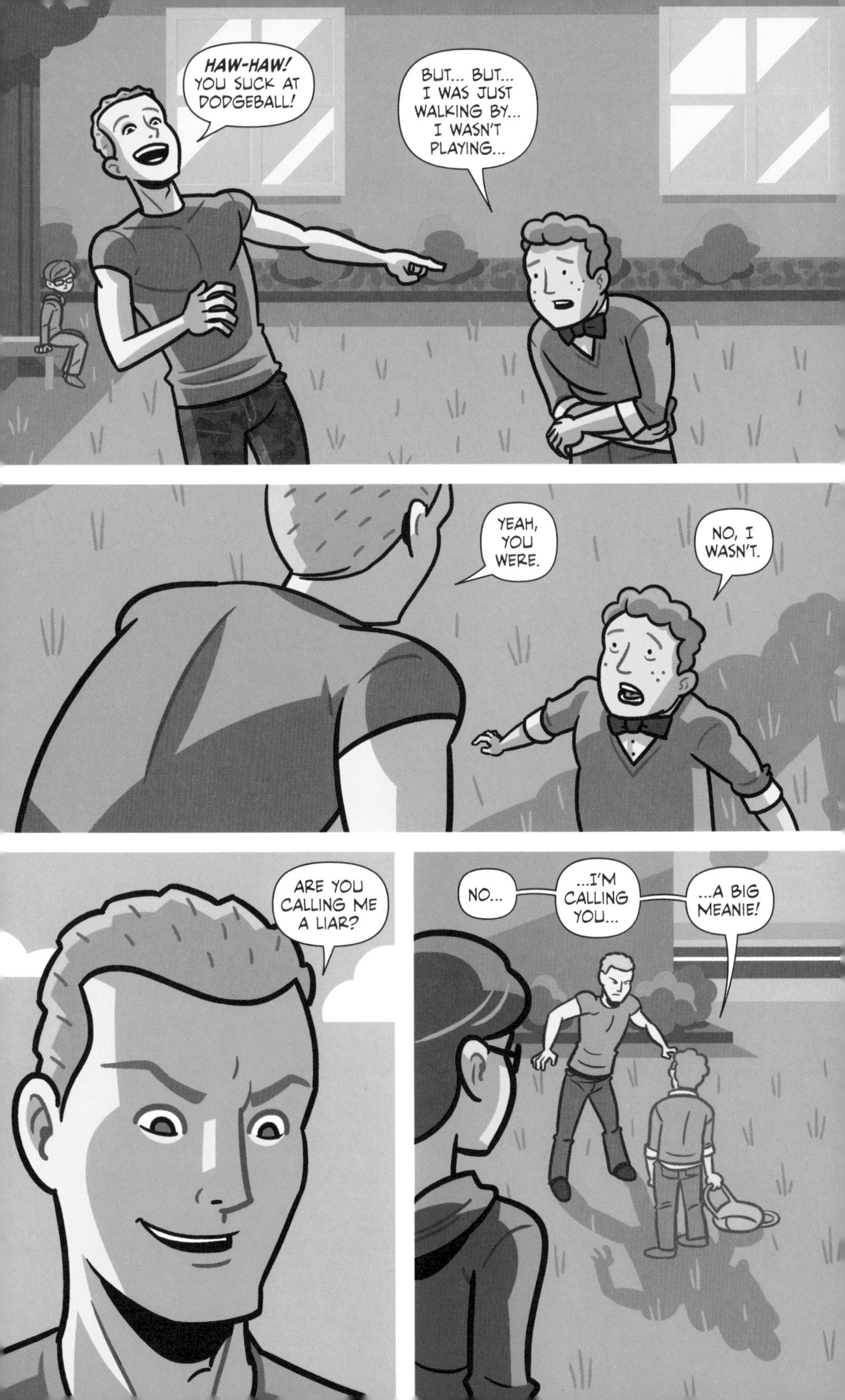
HAW-HAW! YOU SUCK AT DODGEBALL!
BUT... BUT... I WAS JUST WALKING BY... I WASN'T PLAYING...
YEAH, YOU WERE.
NO, I WASN'T.
ARE YOU CALLING ME A LIAR?
NO...
...I'M CALLING YOU...
...A BIG MEANIE!

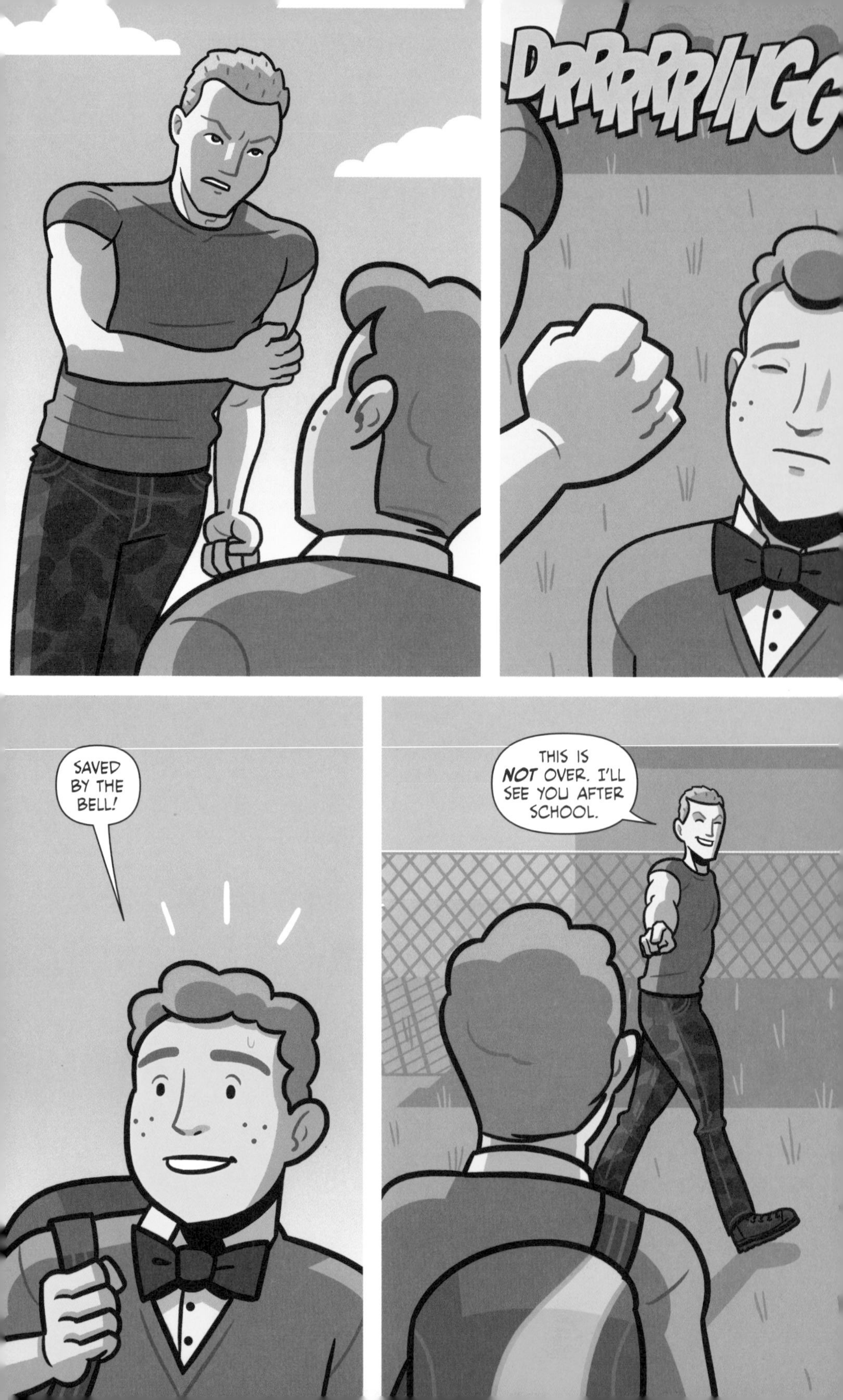

DRRRRRRINGG
SAVED BY THE BELL!
THIS IS NOT OVER. I'LL SEE YOU AFTER SCHOOL.

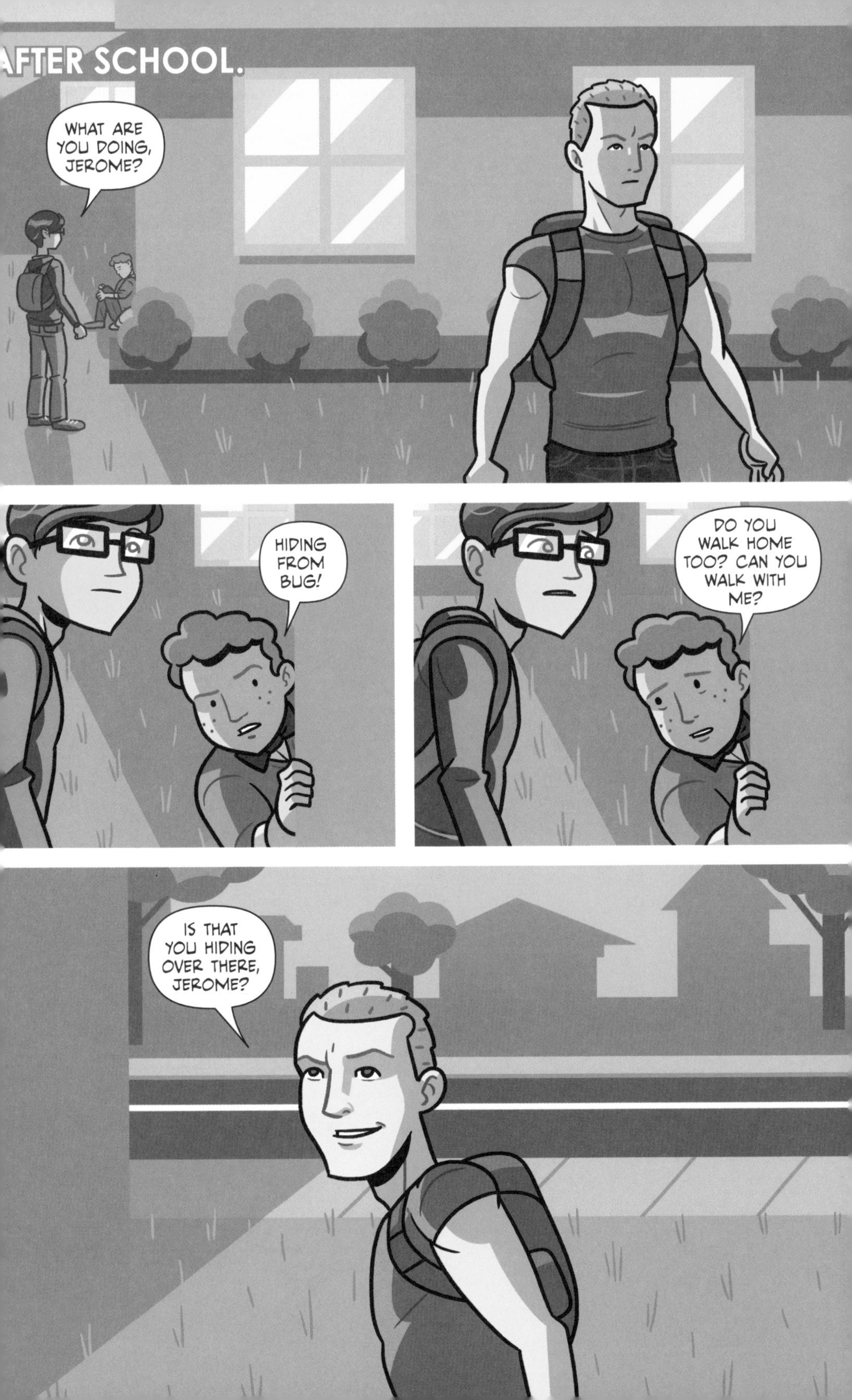
AFTER SCHOOL.
WHAT ARE YOU DOING, JEROME?
HIDING FROM BUG!
DO YOU WALK HOME TOO? CAN YOU WALK WITH ME?
IS THAT YOU HIDING OVER THERE, JEROME?

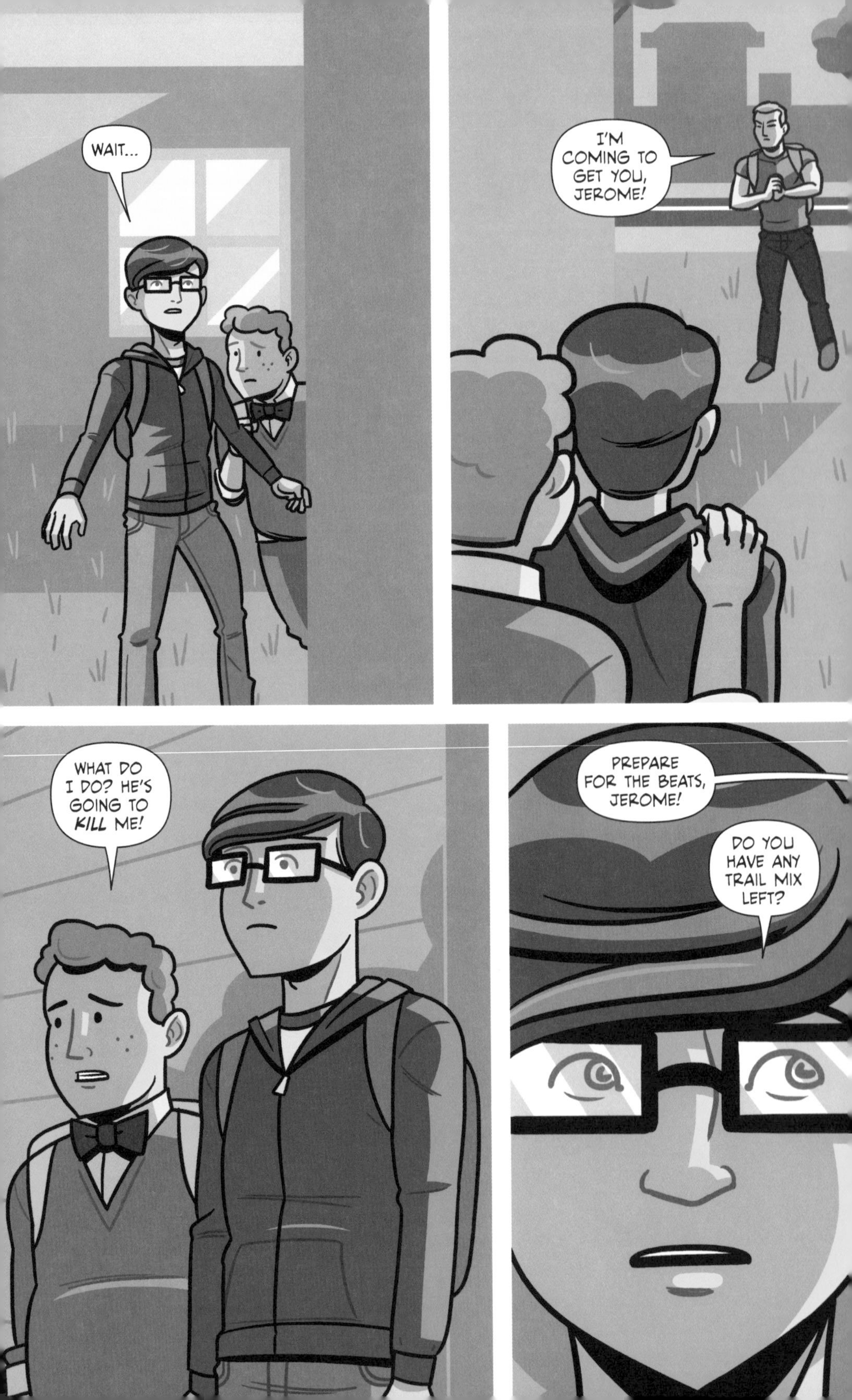
WAIT...
I'M COMING TO GET YOU, JEROME!
WHAT DO I DO? HE'S GOING TO *KILL* ME!
PREPARE FOR THE BEATS, JEROME!
DO YOU HAVE ANY TRAIL MIX LEFT?

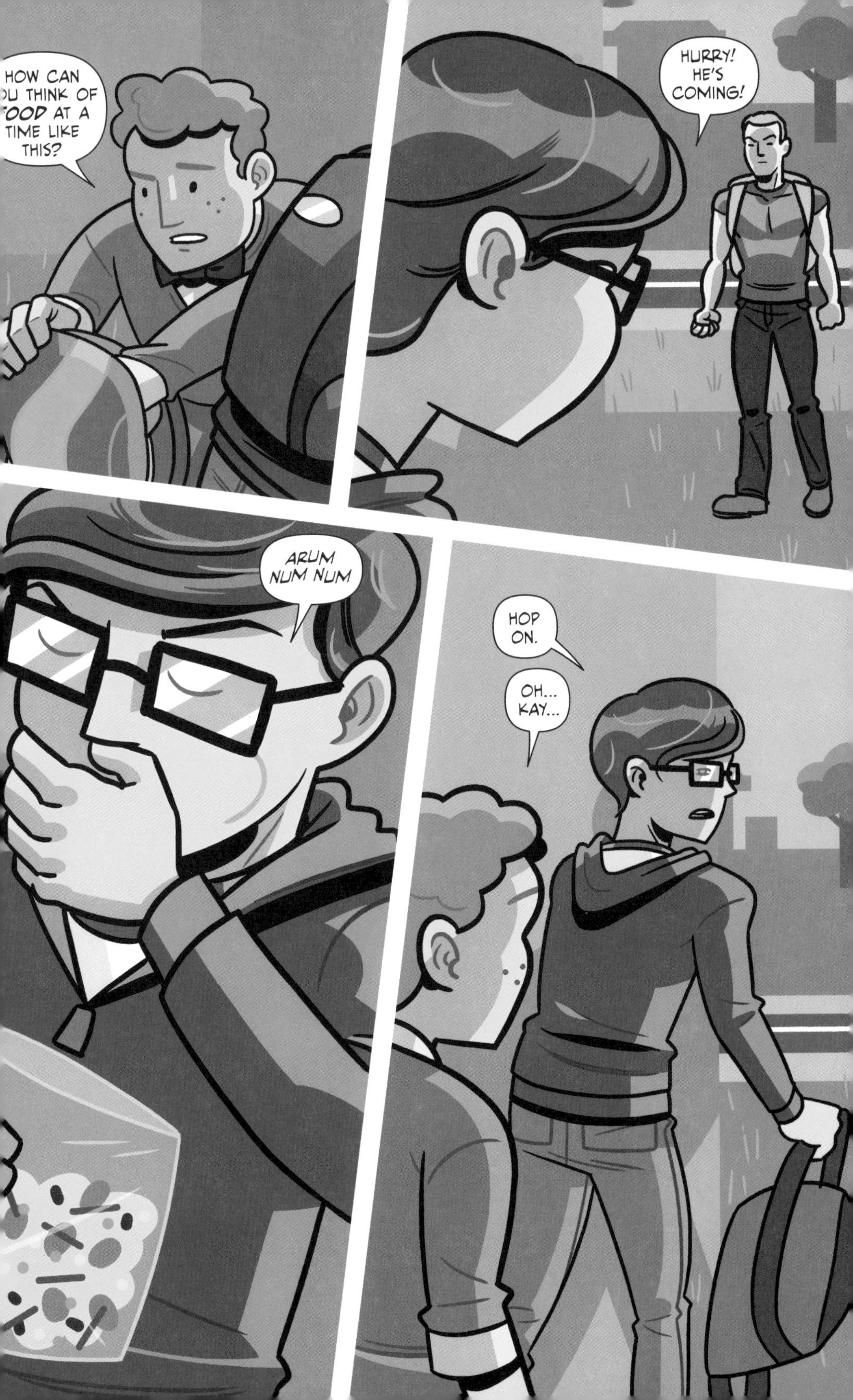
HOW CAN
OU THINK OF
OOD AT A
TIME LIKE
THIS?
HURRY!
HE'S
COMING!
ARUM
NUM NUM
HOP
ON.
OH...
KAY...

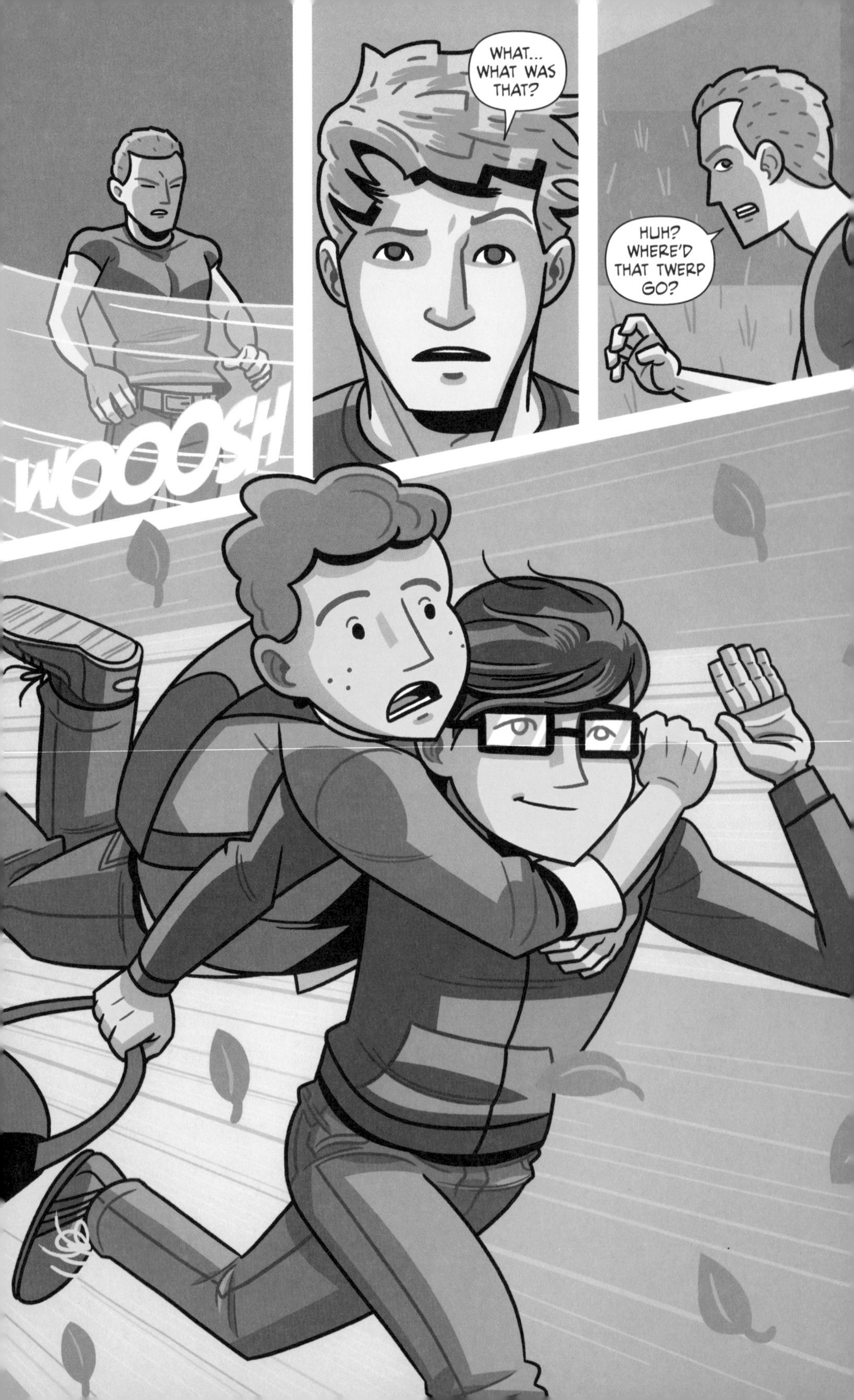
WOOOSH
WHAT... WHAT WAS THAT?
HUH? WHERE'D THAT TWERP GO?

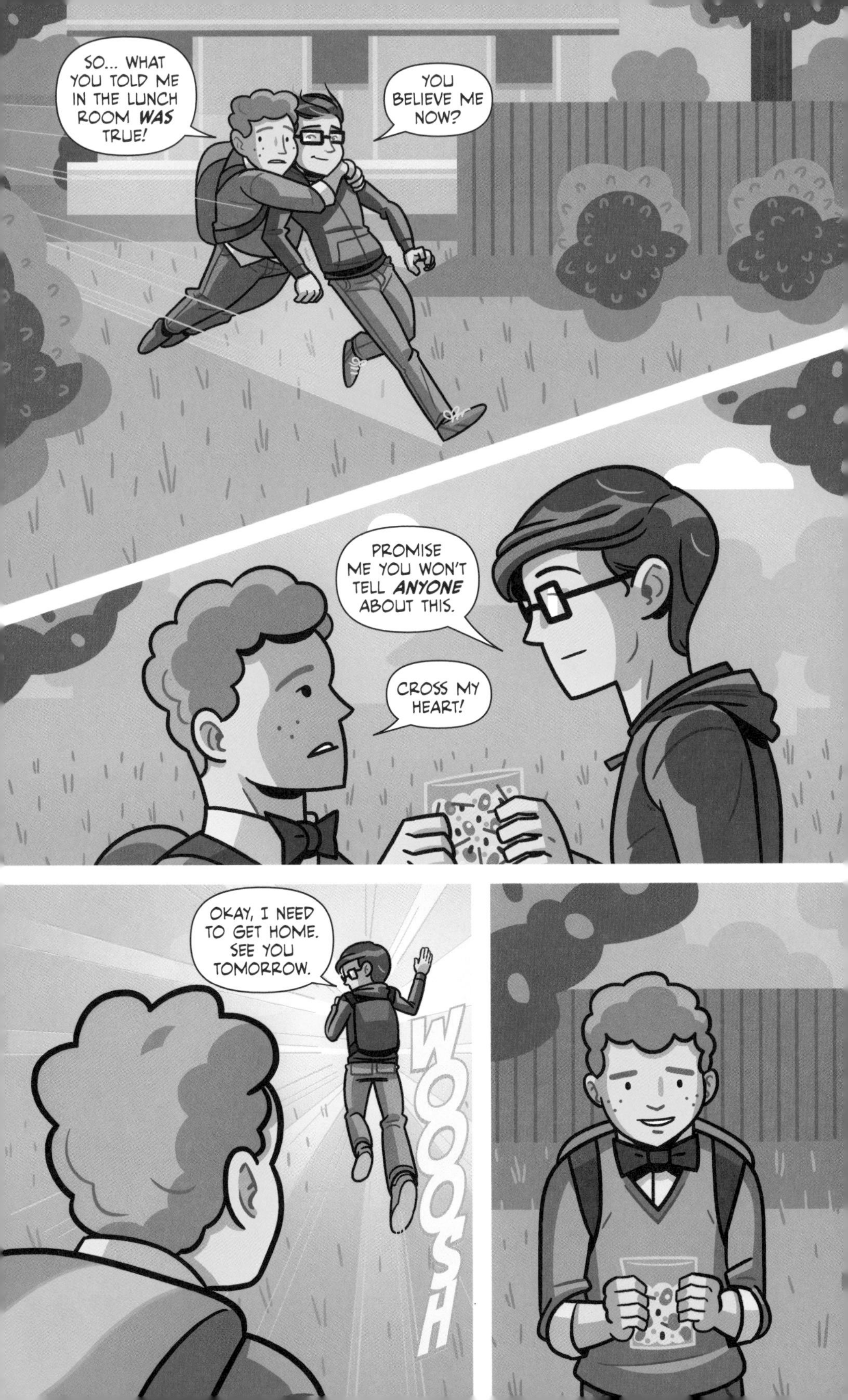
SO... WHAT YOU TOLD ME IN THE LUNCH ROOM WAS TRUE!
YOU BELIEVE ME NOW?
PROMISE ME YOU WON'T TELL ANYONE ABOUT THIS.
CROSS MY HEART!
OKAY, I NEED TO GET HOME. SEE YOU TOMORROW.
WOOOOSH

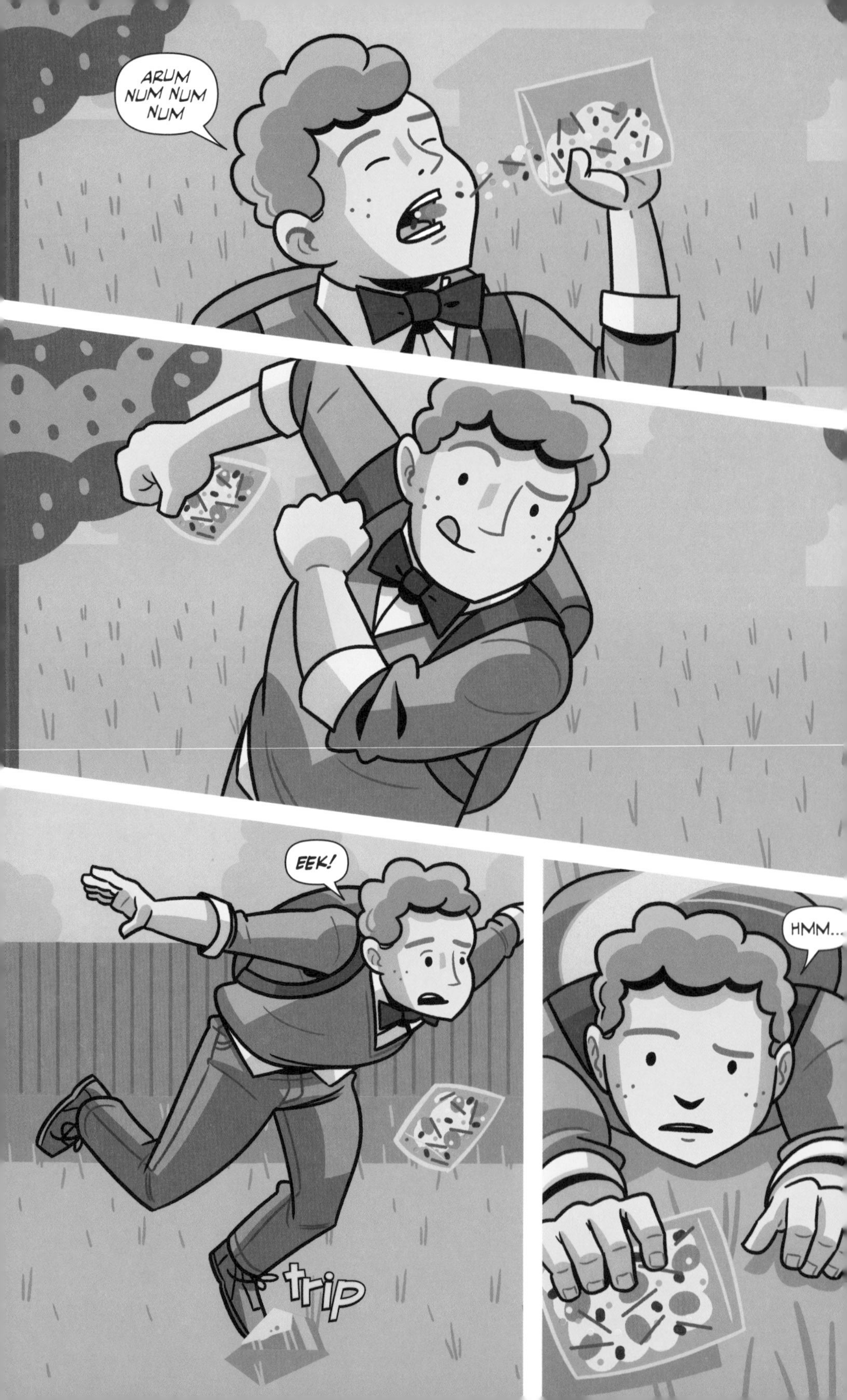
ARUM NUM NUM NUM
EEK!
trip
HMM...

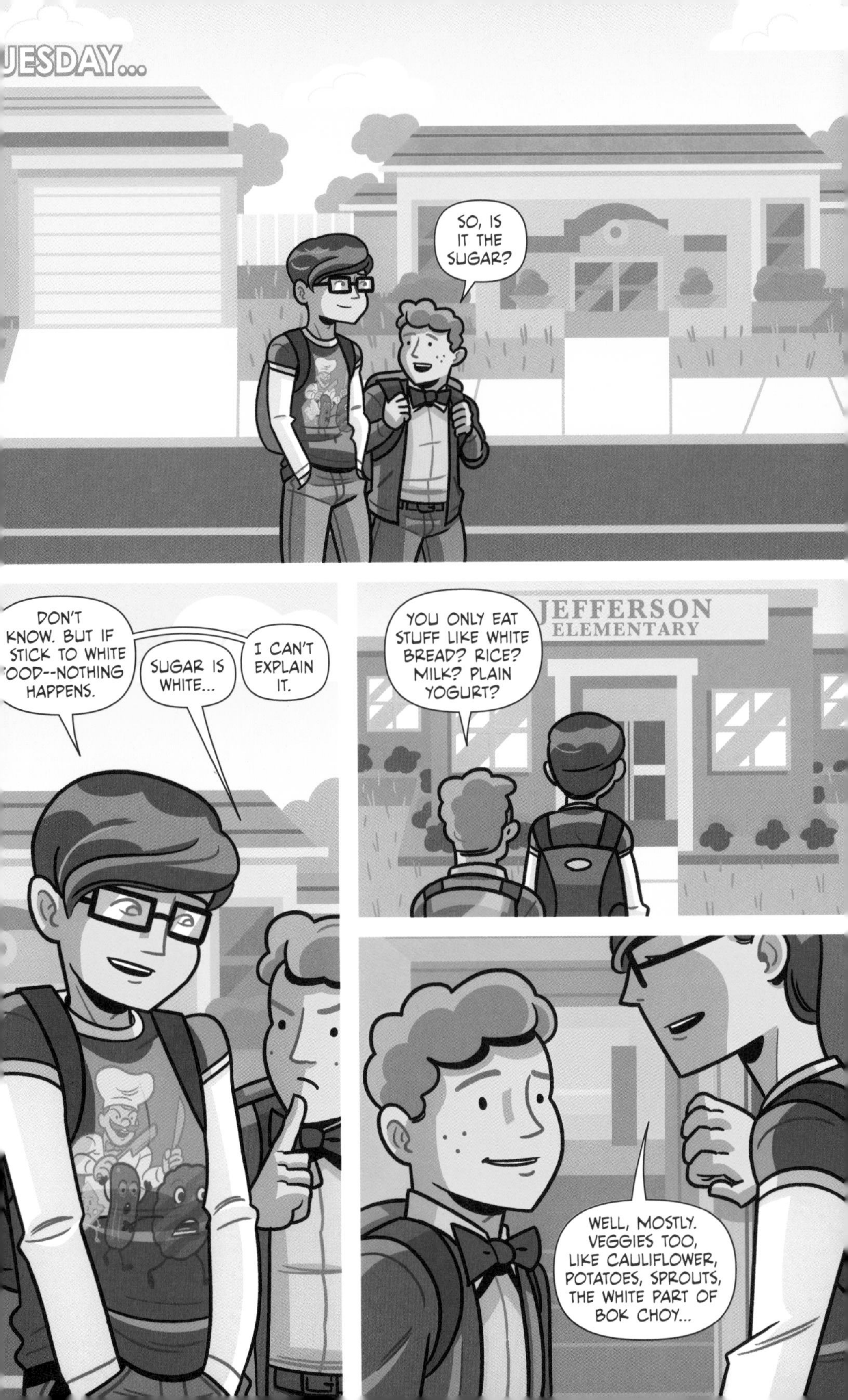
UESDAY...
SO, IS IT THE SUGAR?
DON'T KNOW. BUT IF STICK TO WHITE OOD--NOTHING HAPPENS.
I CAN'T EXPLAIN IT.
SUGAR IS WHITE...
JEFFERSON ELEMENTARY
YOU ONLY EAT STUFF LIKE WHITE BREAD? RICE? MILK? PLAIN YOGURT?
WELL, MOSTLY. VEGGIES TOO, LIKE CAULIFLOWER, POTATOES, SPROUTS, THE WHITE PART OF BOK CHOY...

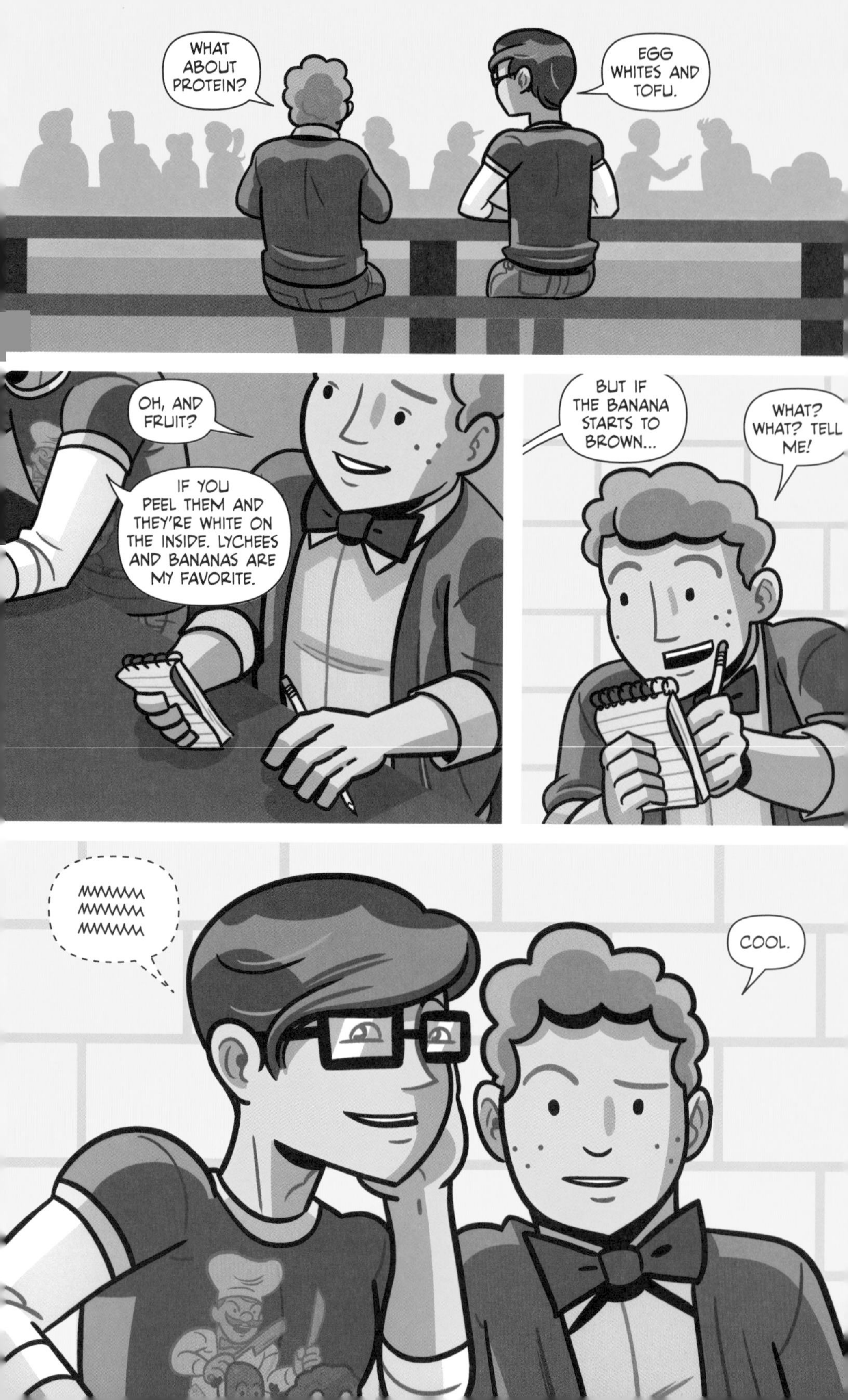
WHAT ABOUT PROTEIN?
EGG WHITES AND TOFU.
OH, AND FRUIT?
IF YOU PEEL THEM AND THEY'RE WHITE ON THE INSIDE. LYCHEES AND BANANAS ARE MY FAVORITE.
BUT IF THE BANANA STARTS TO BROWN...
WHAT? WHAT? TELL ME!
COOL.

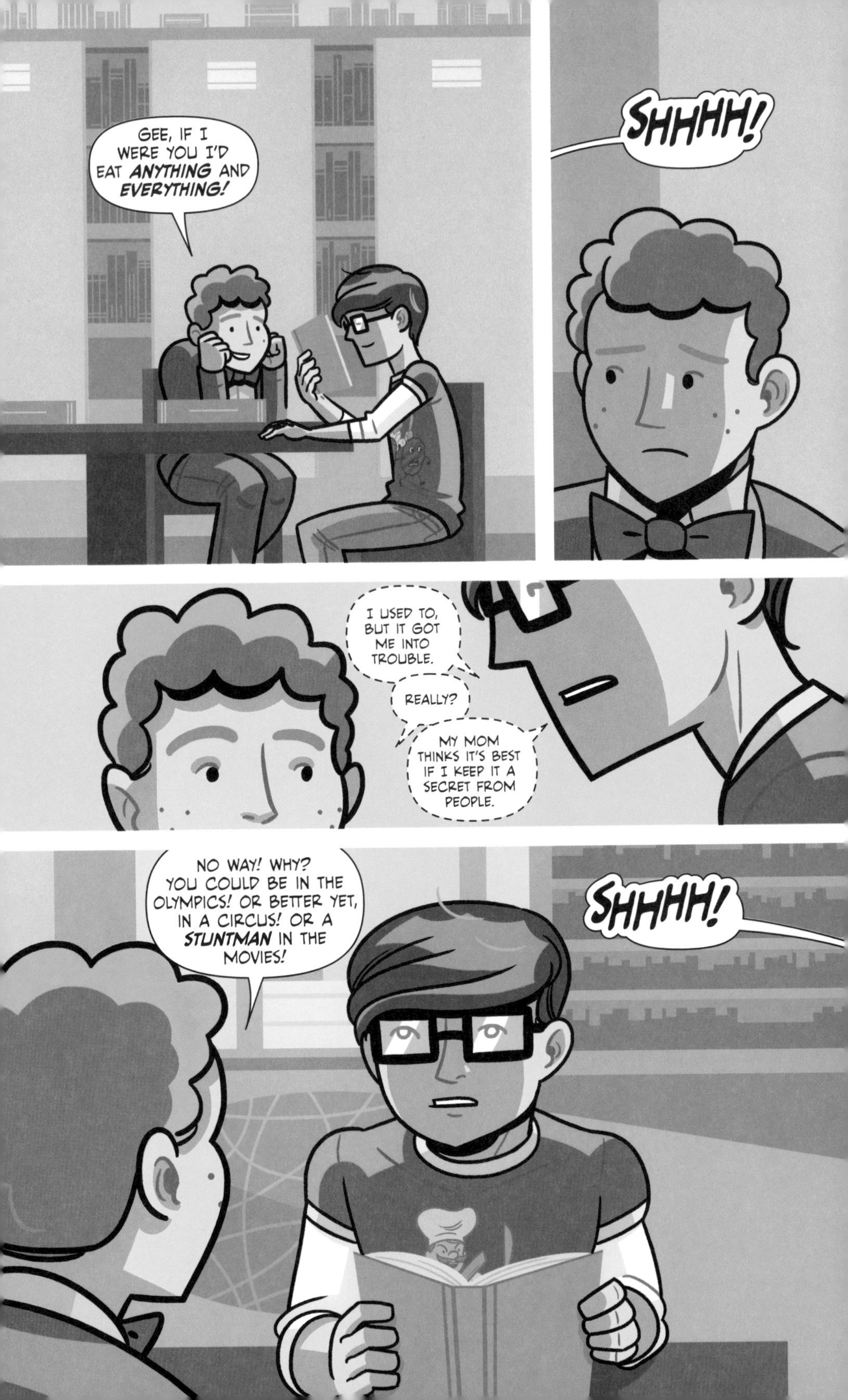
GEE, IF I WERE YOU I'D EAT ANYTHING AND EVERYTHING!
SHHHH!
I USED TO, BUT IT GOT ME INTO TROUBLE.
REALLY?
MY MOM THINKS IT'S BEST IF I KEEP IT A SECRET FROM PEOPLE.
NO WAY! WHY? YOU COULD BE IN THE OLYMPICS! OR BETTER YET, IN A CIRCUS! OR A STUNTMAN IN THE MOVIES!
SHHHH!

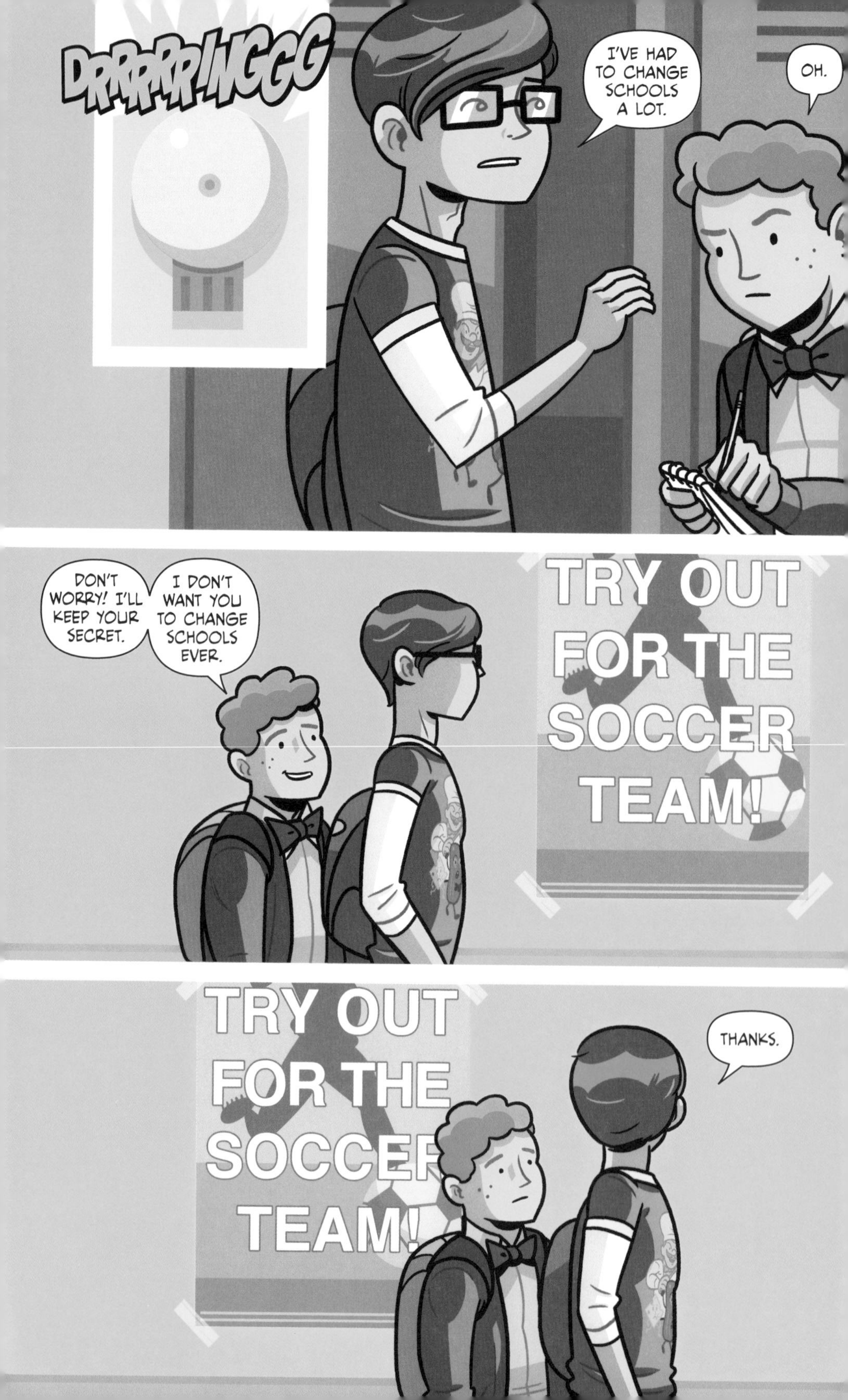
DRRRRRINGGG
I'VE HAD TO CHANGE SCHOOLS A LOT.
OH.
DON'T WORRY! I'LL KEEP YOUR SECRET.
I DON'T WANT YOU TO CHANGE SCHOOLS EVER.
TRY OUT FOR THE SOCCER TEAM!
TRY OUT FOR THE SOCCER TEAM!
THANKS.

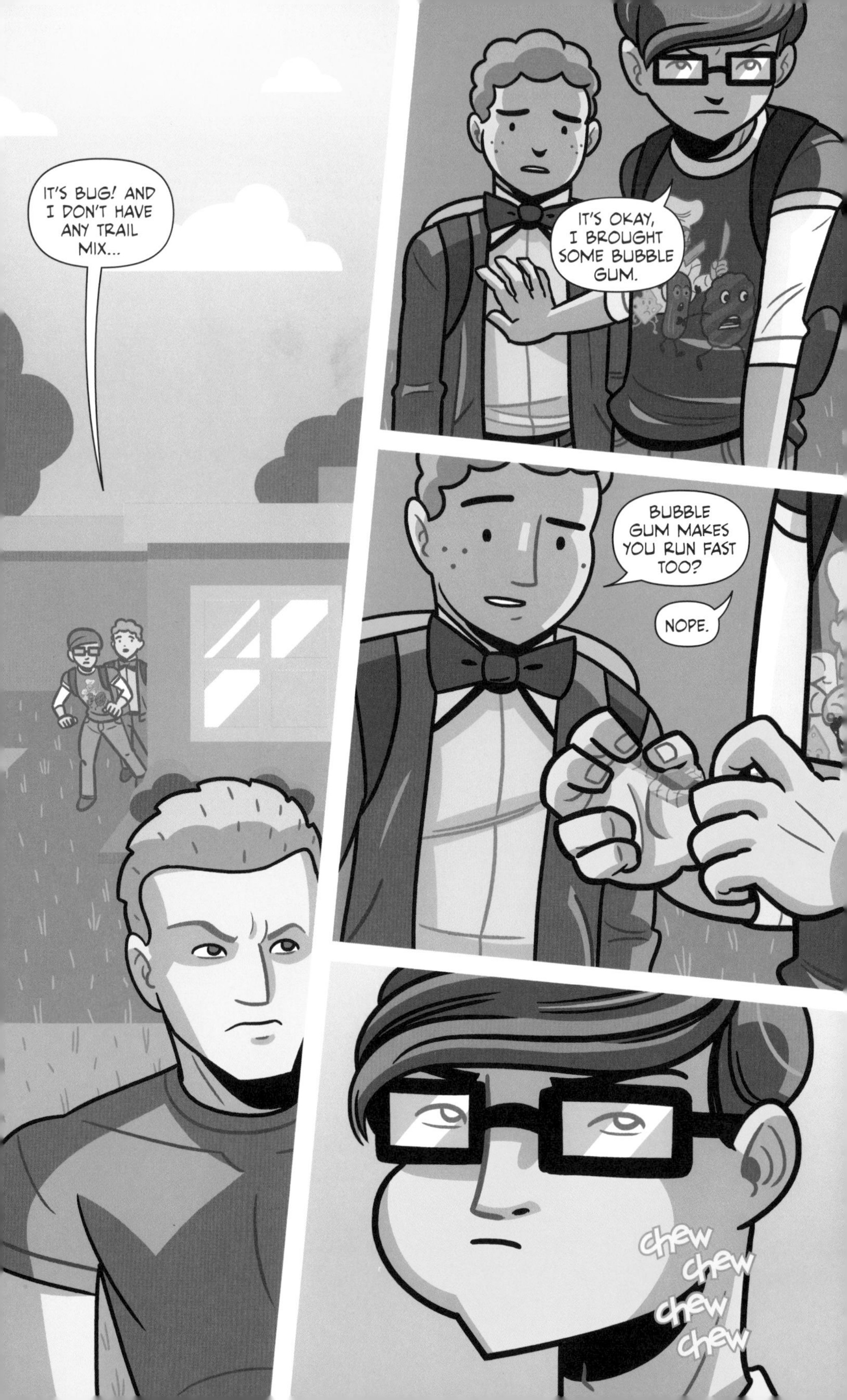
IT'S BUG! AND I DON'T HAVE ANY TRAIL MIX...
IT'S OKAY, I BROUGHT SOME BUBBLE GUM.
BUBBLE GUM MAKES YOU RUN FAST TOO?
NOPE.
chew chew chew chew

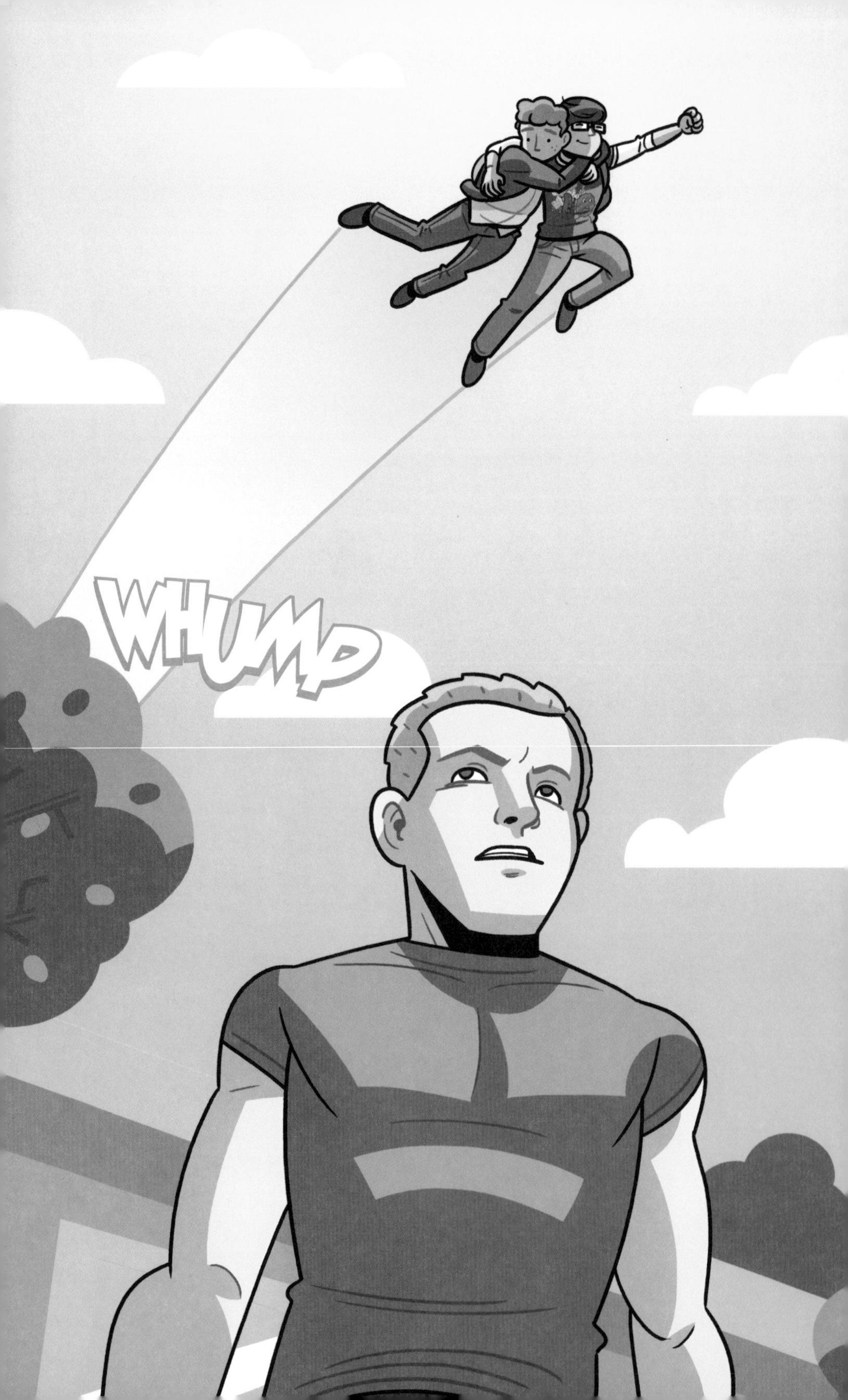
WHUMP

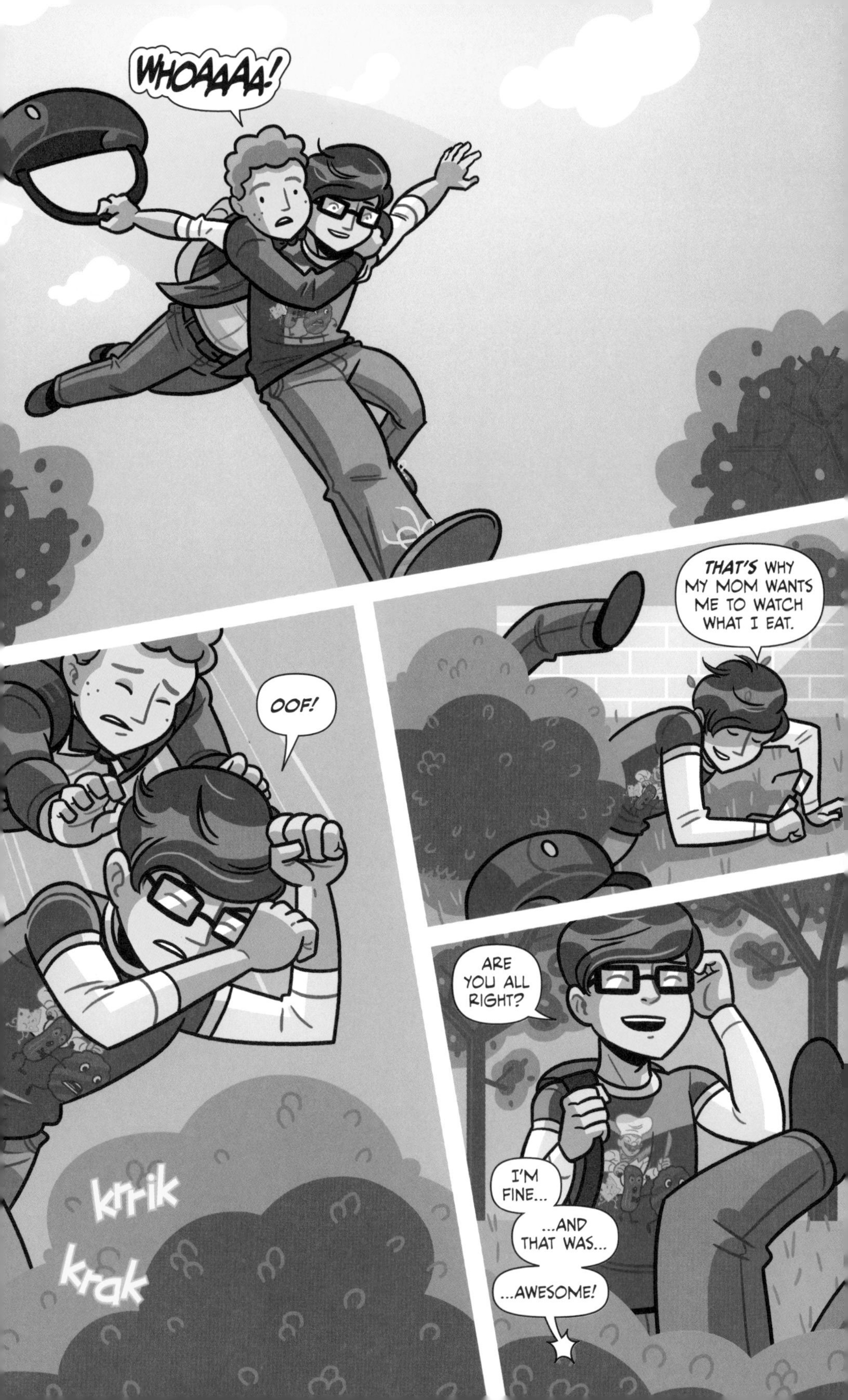
WHOAAAA!
OOF!
krrik
krak
THAT'S WHY MY MOM WANTS ME TO WATCH WHAT I EAT.
ARE YOU ALL RIGHT?
I'M FINE...
...AND THAT WAS...
...AWESOME!

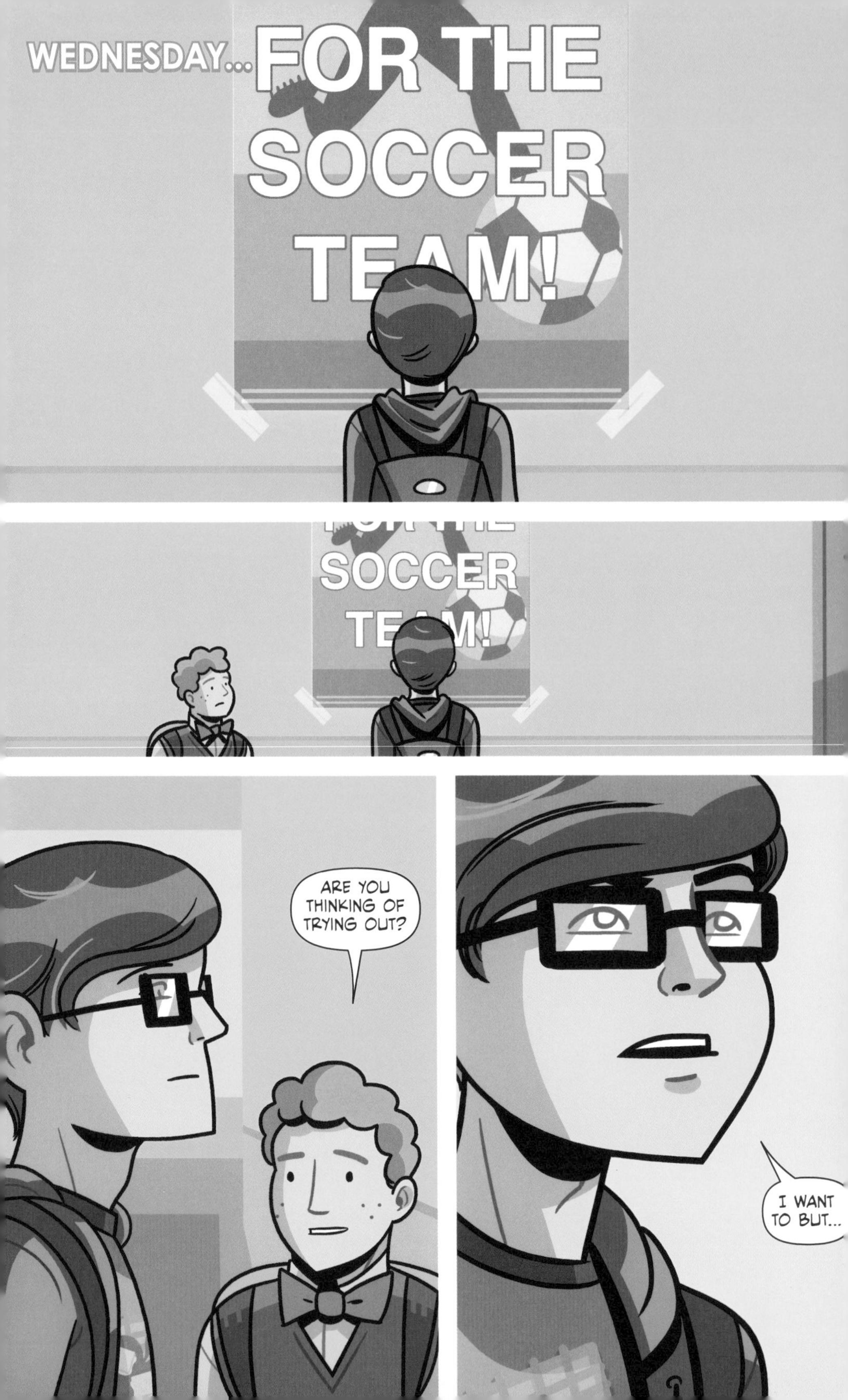
WEDNESDAY...
FOR THE SOCCER TEAM!
FOR THE SOCCER TEAM!
ARE YOU THINKING OF TRYING OUT?
I WANT TO BUT...

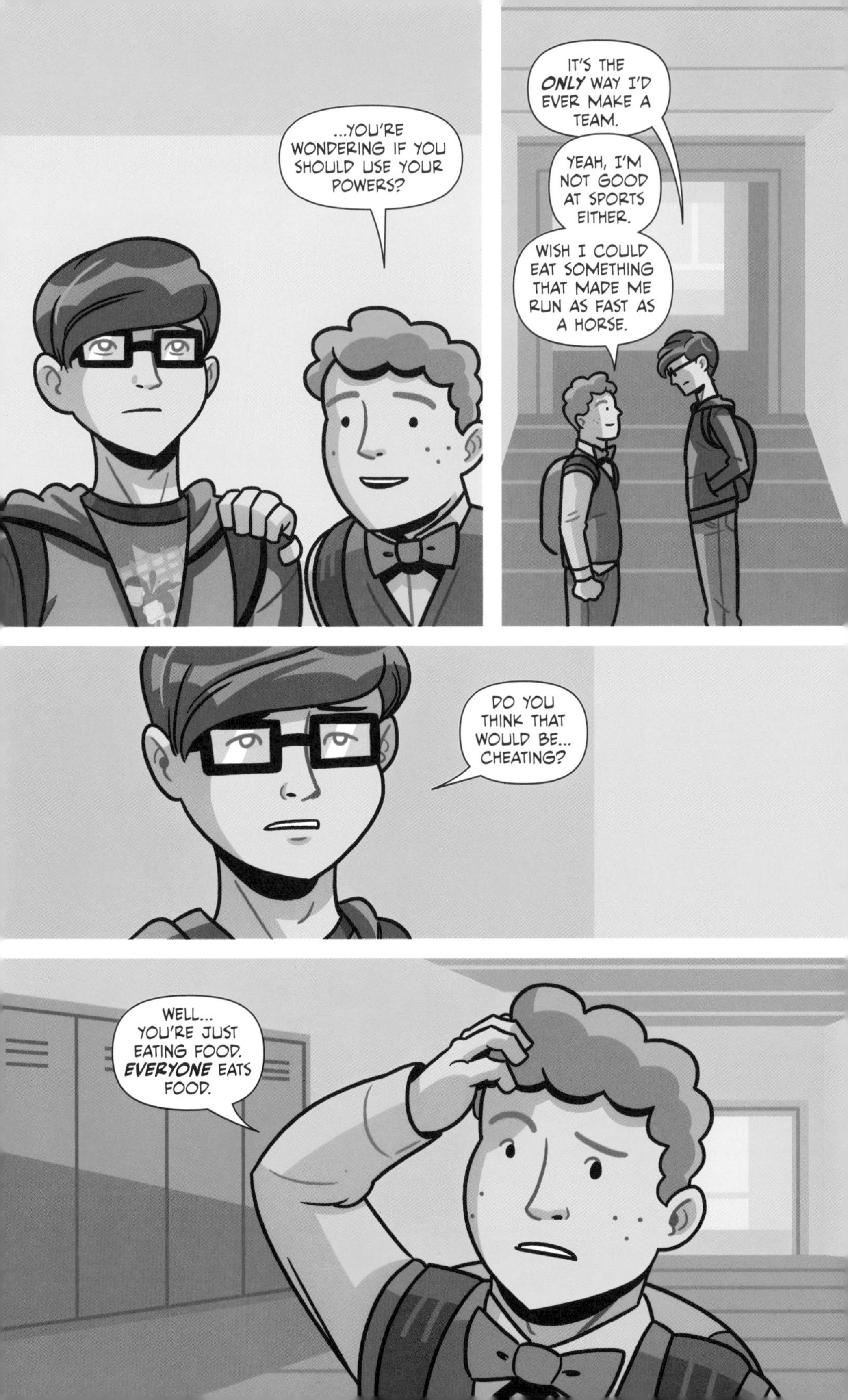
...YOU'RE WONDERING IF YOU SHOULD USE YOUR POWERS?
IT'S THE ONLY WAY I'D EVER MAKE A TEAM.
YEAH, I'M NOT GOOD AT SPORTS EITHER.
WISH I COULD EAT SOMETHING THAT MADE ME RUN AS FAST AS A HORSE.
DO YOU THINK THAT WOULD BE... CHEATING?
WELL... YOU'RE JUST EATING FOOD. EVERYONE EATS FOOD.

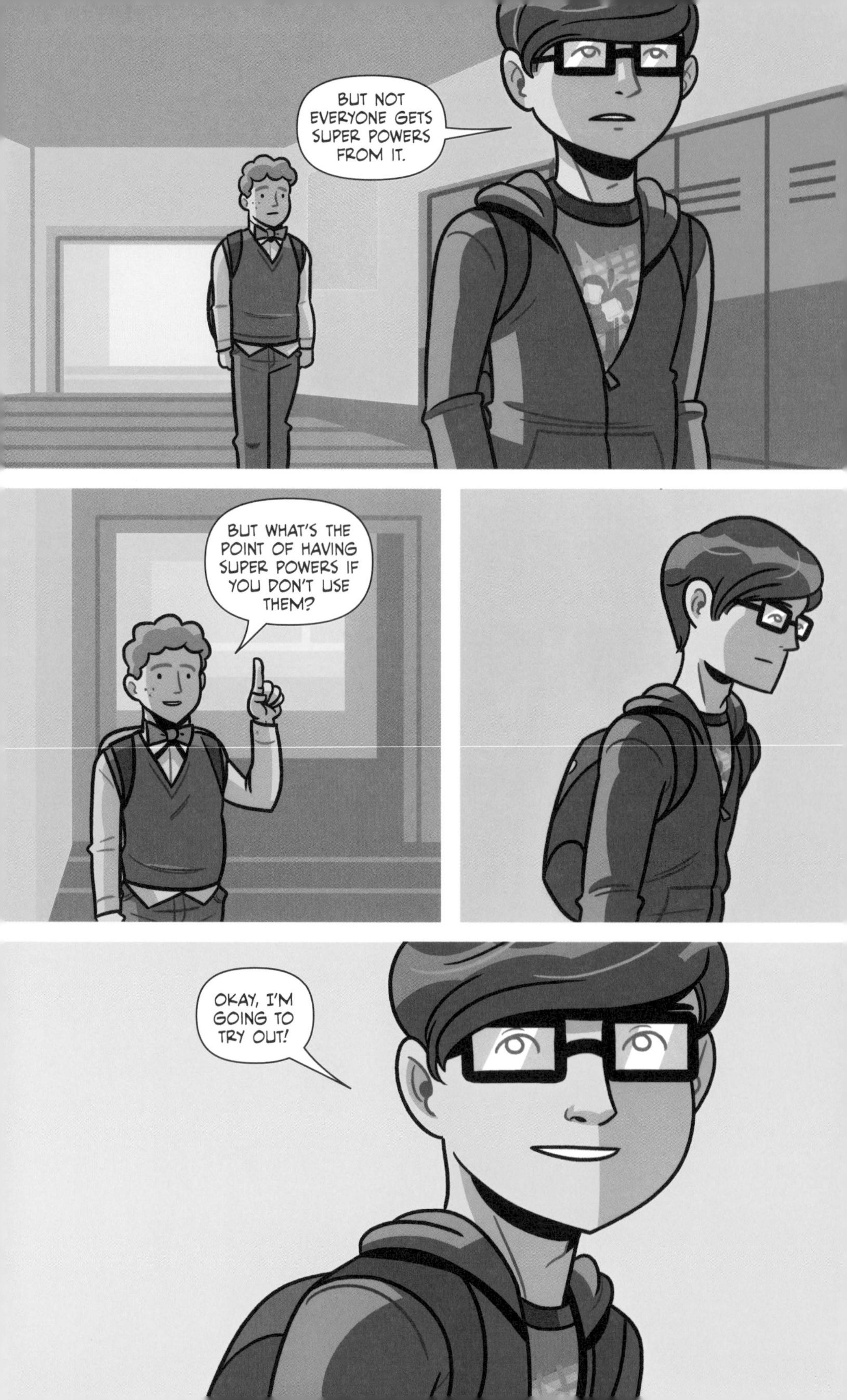
BUT NOT EVERYONE GETS SUPER POWERS FROM IT.
BUT WHAT'S THE POINT OF HAVING SUPER POWERS IF YOU DON'T USE THEM?
OKAY, I'M GOING TO TRY OUT!

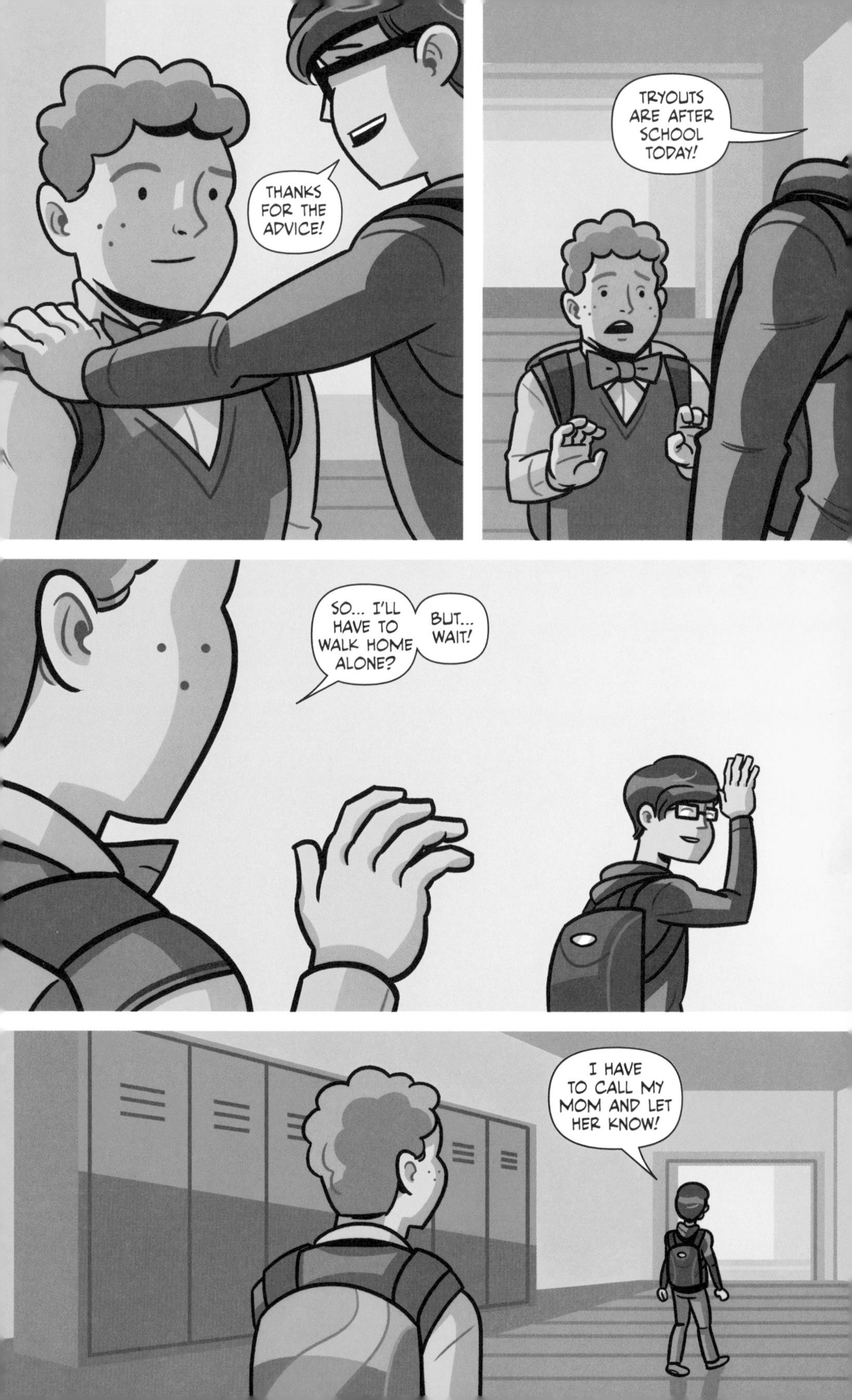
THANKS FOR THE ADVICE!
TRYOUTS ARE AFTER SCHOOL TODAY!
SO... I'LL HAVE TO WALK HOME ALONE?
BUT... WAIT!
I HAVE TO CALL MY MOM AND LET HER KNOW!

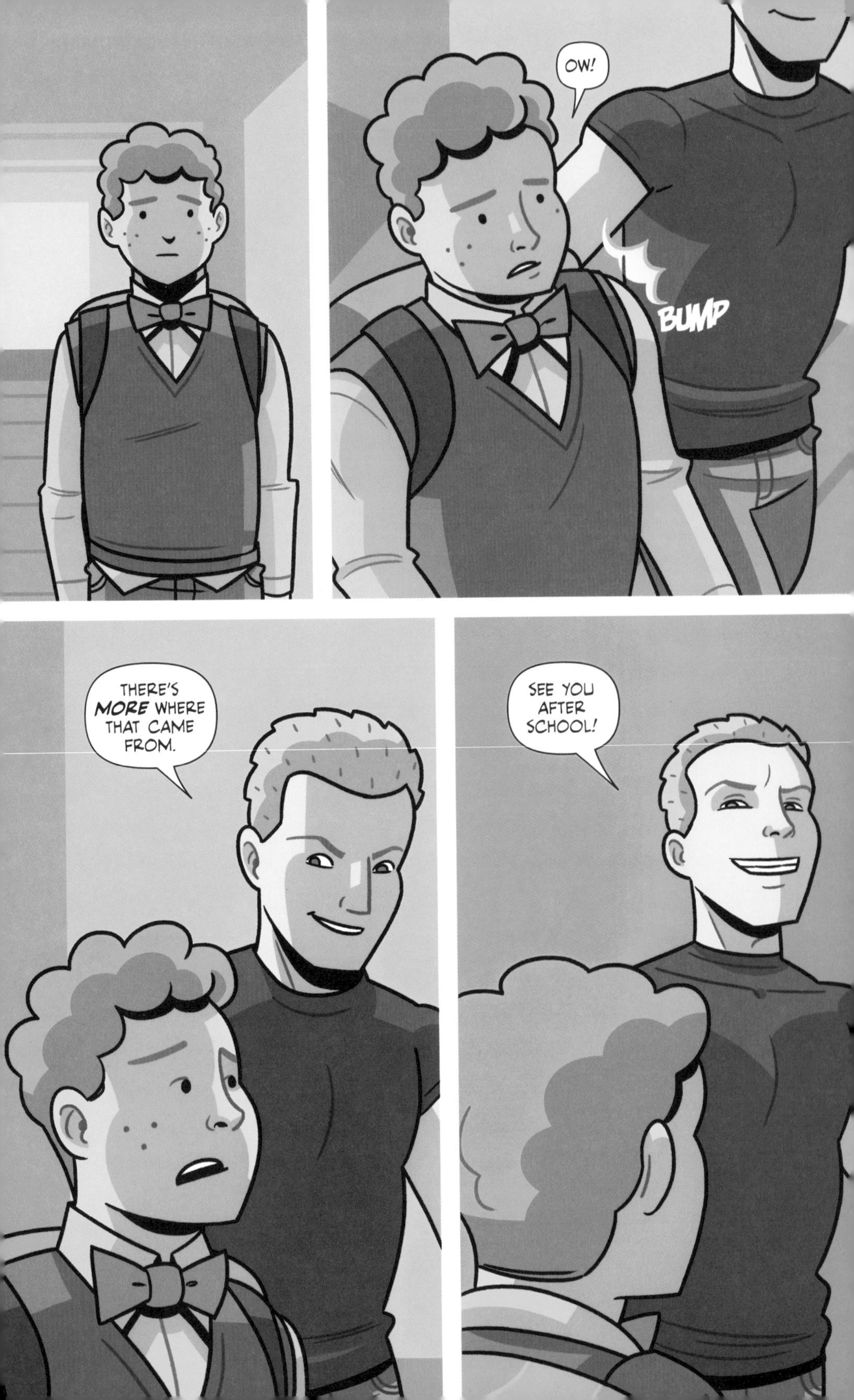
OW!
BUMP
THERE'S **MORE** WHERE THAT CAME FROM.
SEE YOU AFTER SCHOOL!

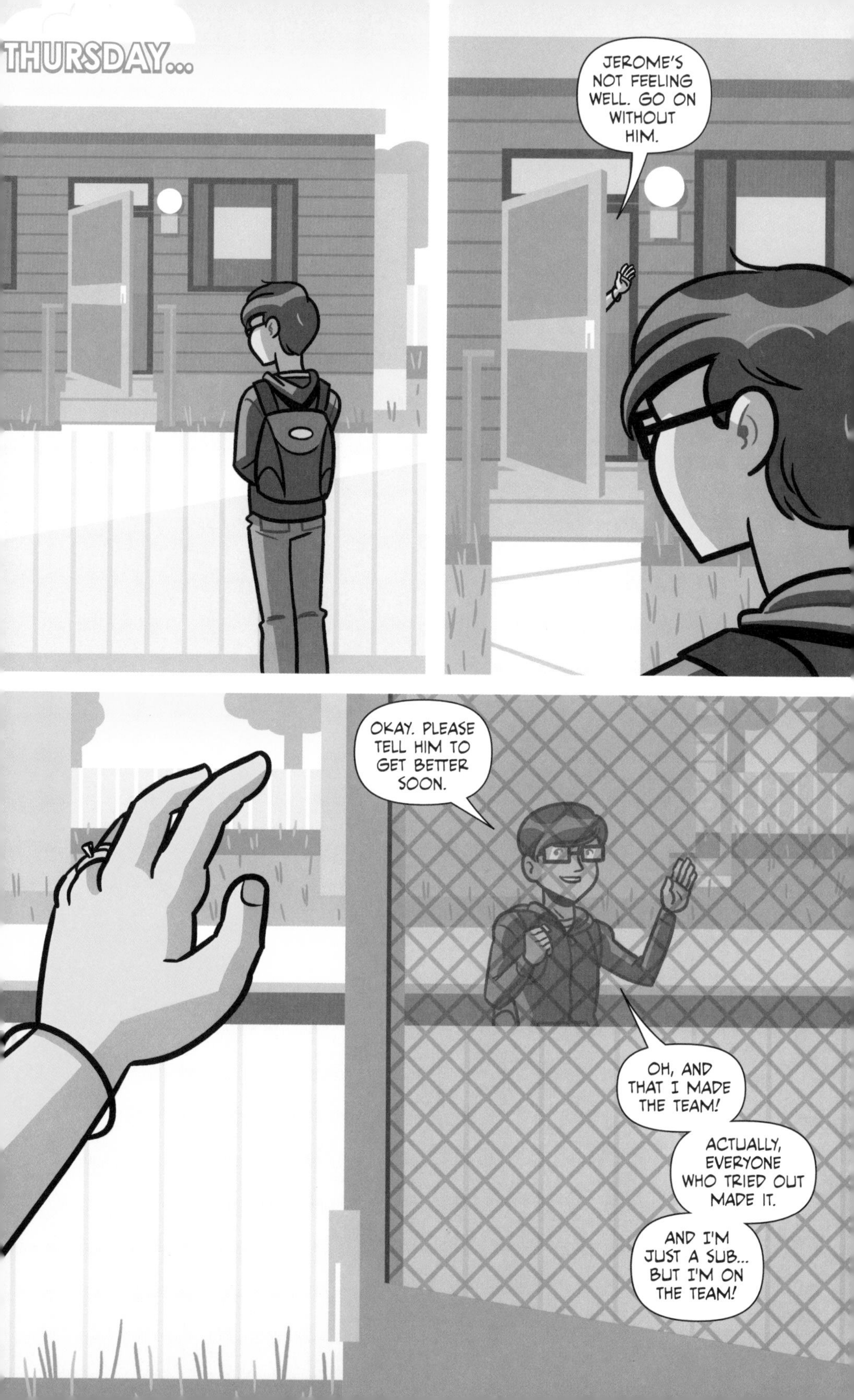
THURSDAY...
JEROME'S NOT FEELING WELL. GO ON WITHOUT HIM.
OKAY. PLEASE TELL HIM TO GET BETTER SOON.
OH, AND THAT I MADE THE TEAM!
ACTUALLY, EVERYONE WHO TRIED OUT MADE IT.
AND I'M JUST A SUB... BUT I'M ON THE TEAM!

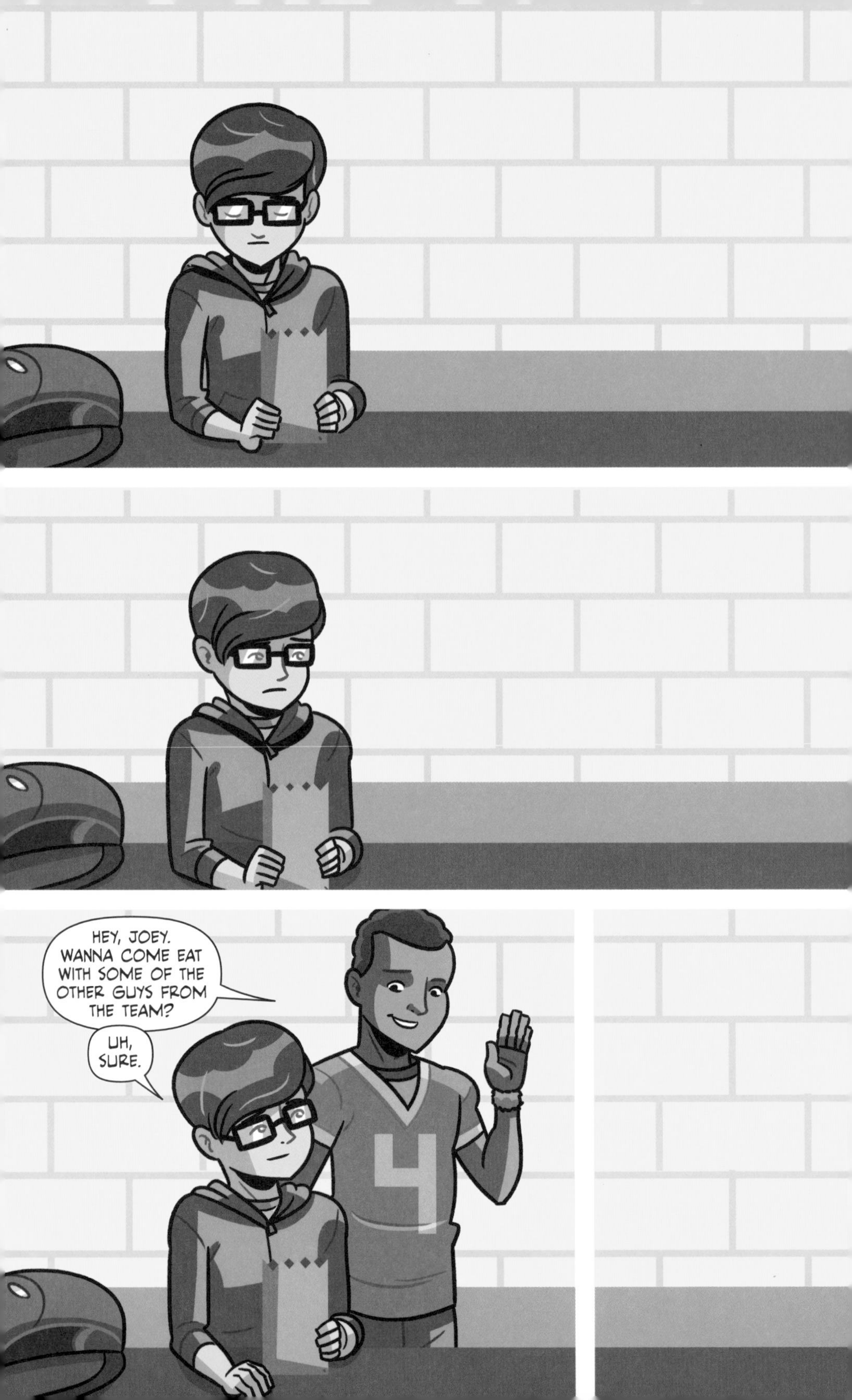
HEY, JOEY. WANNA COME EAT WITH SOME OF THE OTHER GUYS FROM THE TEAM?
UH, SURE.

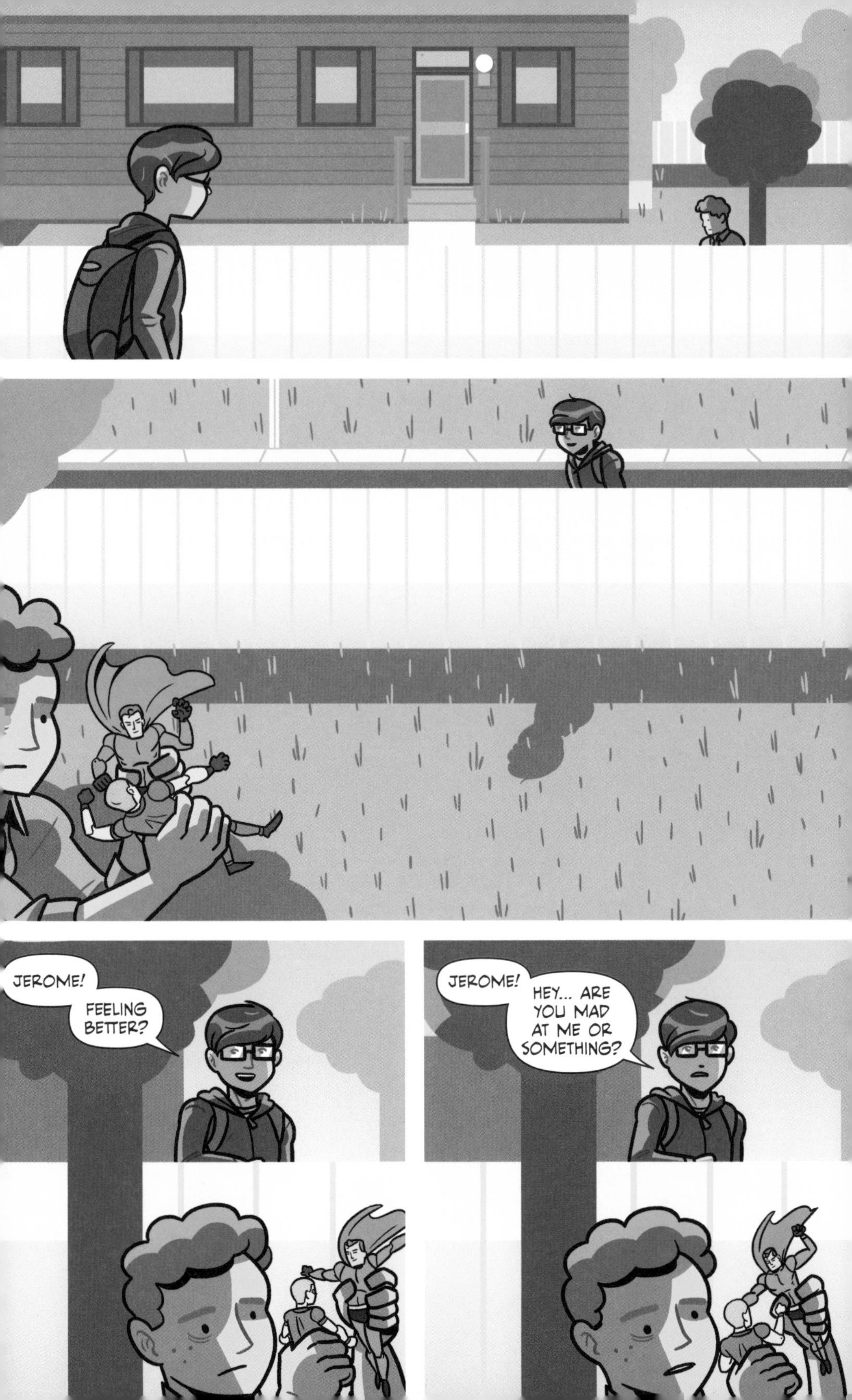
JEROME!
FEELING BETTER?
JEROME!
HEY... ARE YOU MAD AT ME OR SOMETHING?

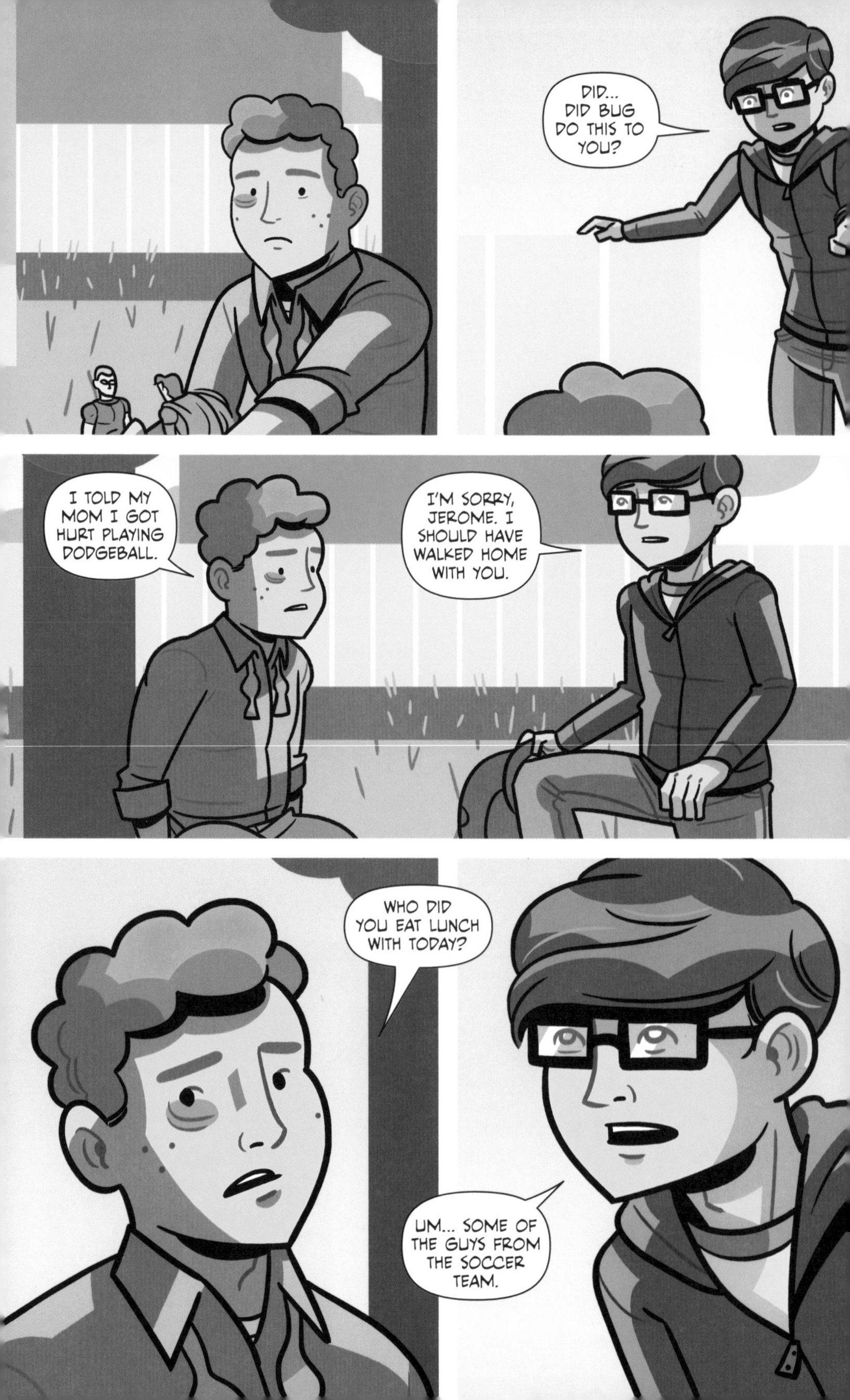
DID... DID BUG DO THIS TO YOU?
I TOLD MY MOM I GOT HURT PLAYING DODGEBALL.
I'M SORRY, JEROME. I SHOULD HAVE WALKED HOME WITH YOU.
WHO DID YOU EAT LUNCH WITH TODAY?
UM... SOME OF THE GUYS FROM THE SOCCER TEAM.

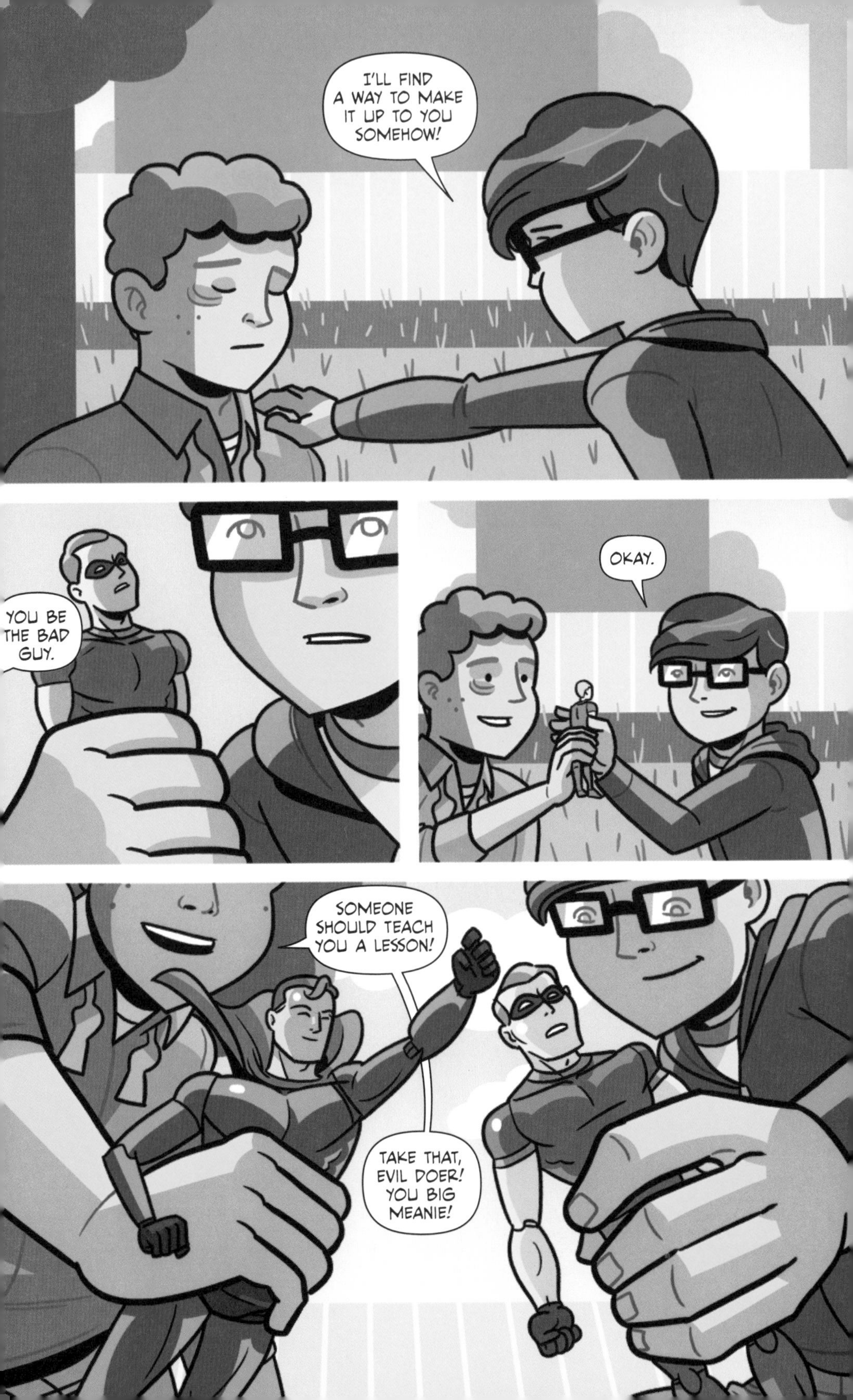
I'LL FIND A WAY TO MAKE IT UP TO YOU SOMEHOW!
YOU BE THE BAD GUY.
OKAY.
SOMEONE SHOULD TEACH YOU A LESSON!
TAKE THAT, EVIL DOER! YOU BIG MEANIE!

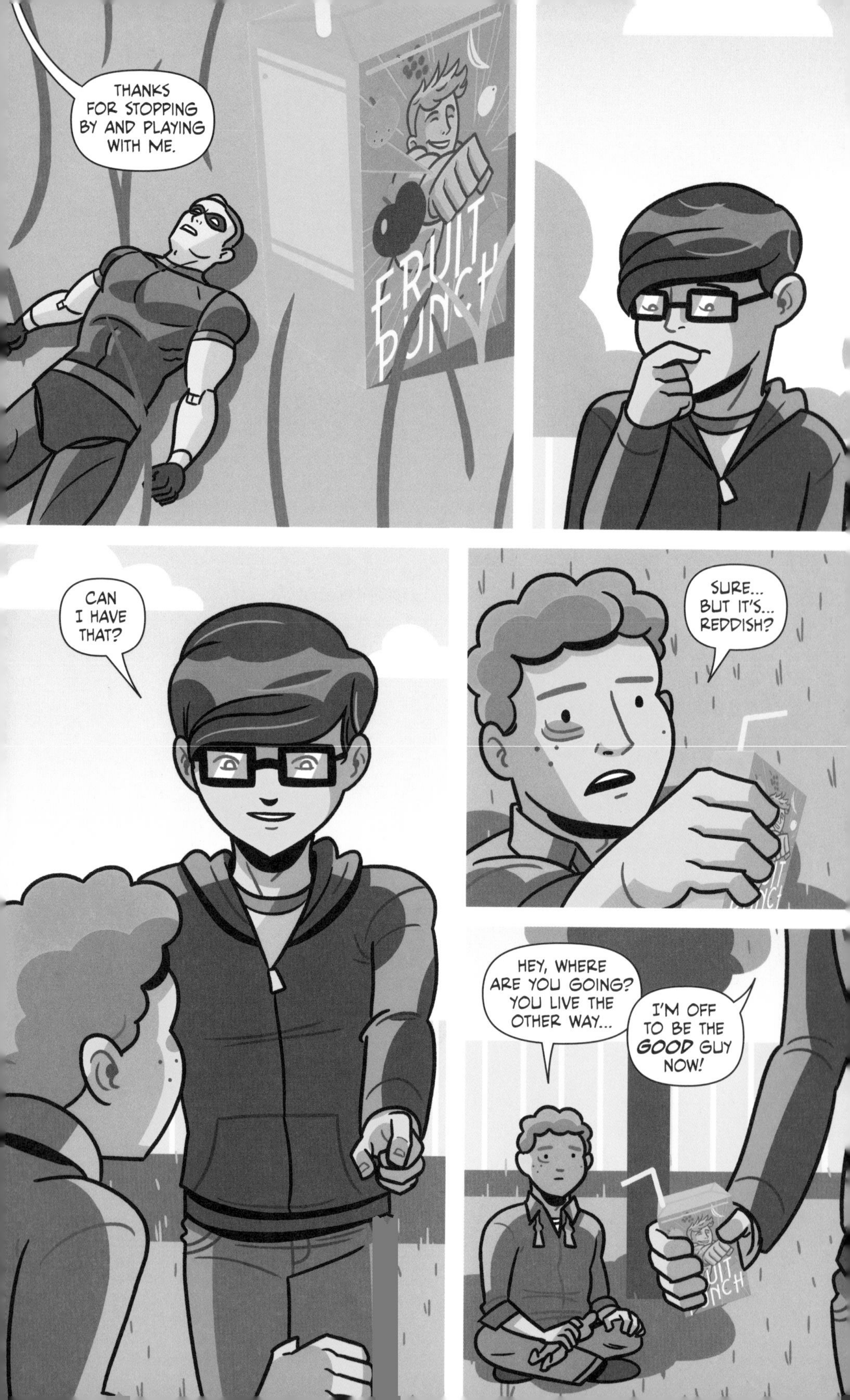
THANKS FOR STOPPING BY AND PLAYING WITH ME.
FRUIT PUNCH
CAN I HAVE THAT?
SURE... BUT IT'S... REDDISH?
HEY, WHERE ARE YOU GOING? YOU LIVE THE OTHER WAY...
I'M OFF TO BE THE **GOOD** GUY NOW!

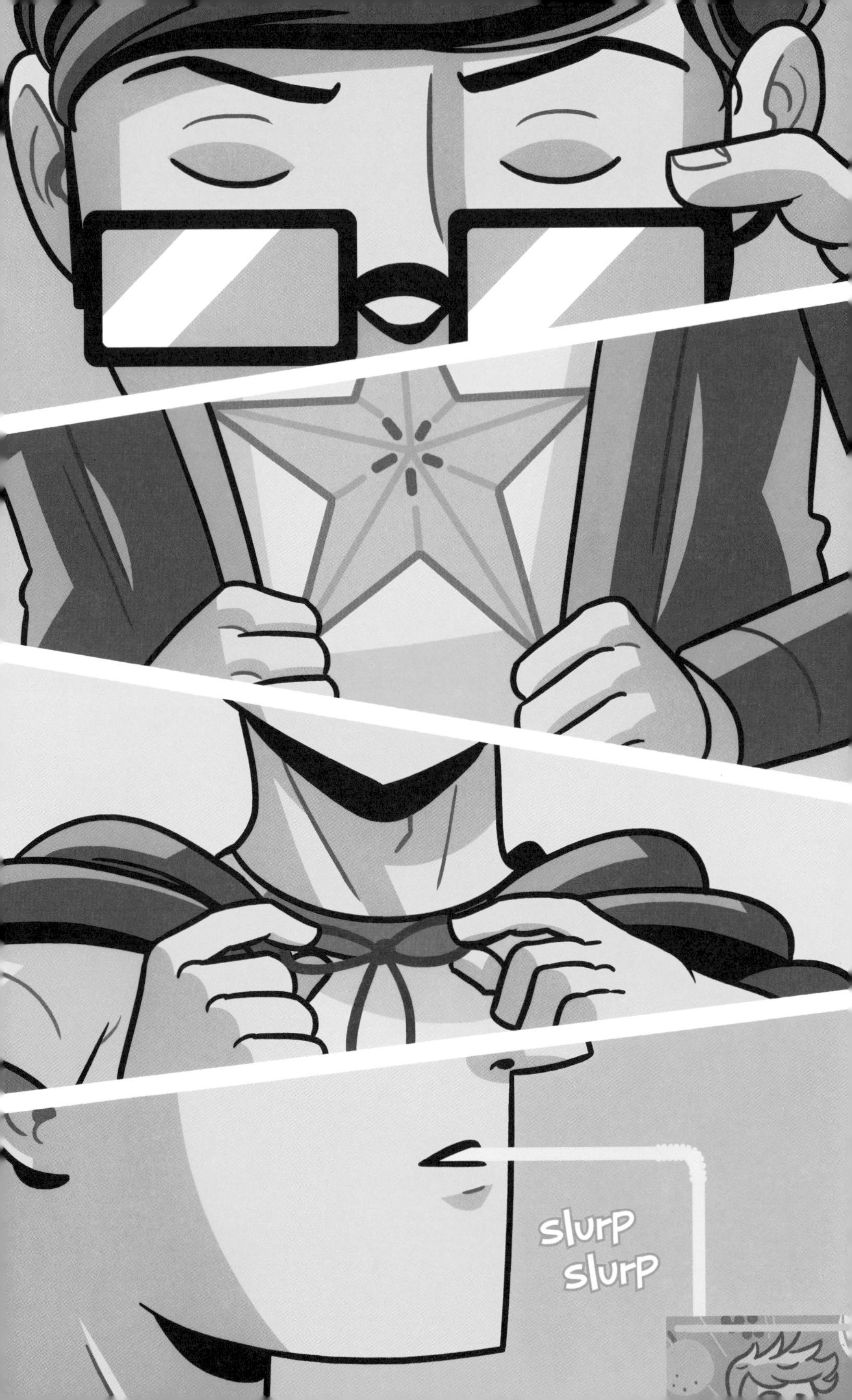
slurp
slurp

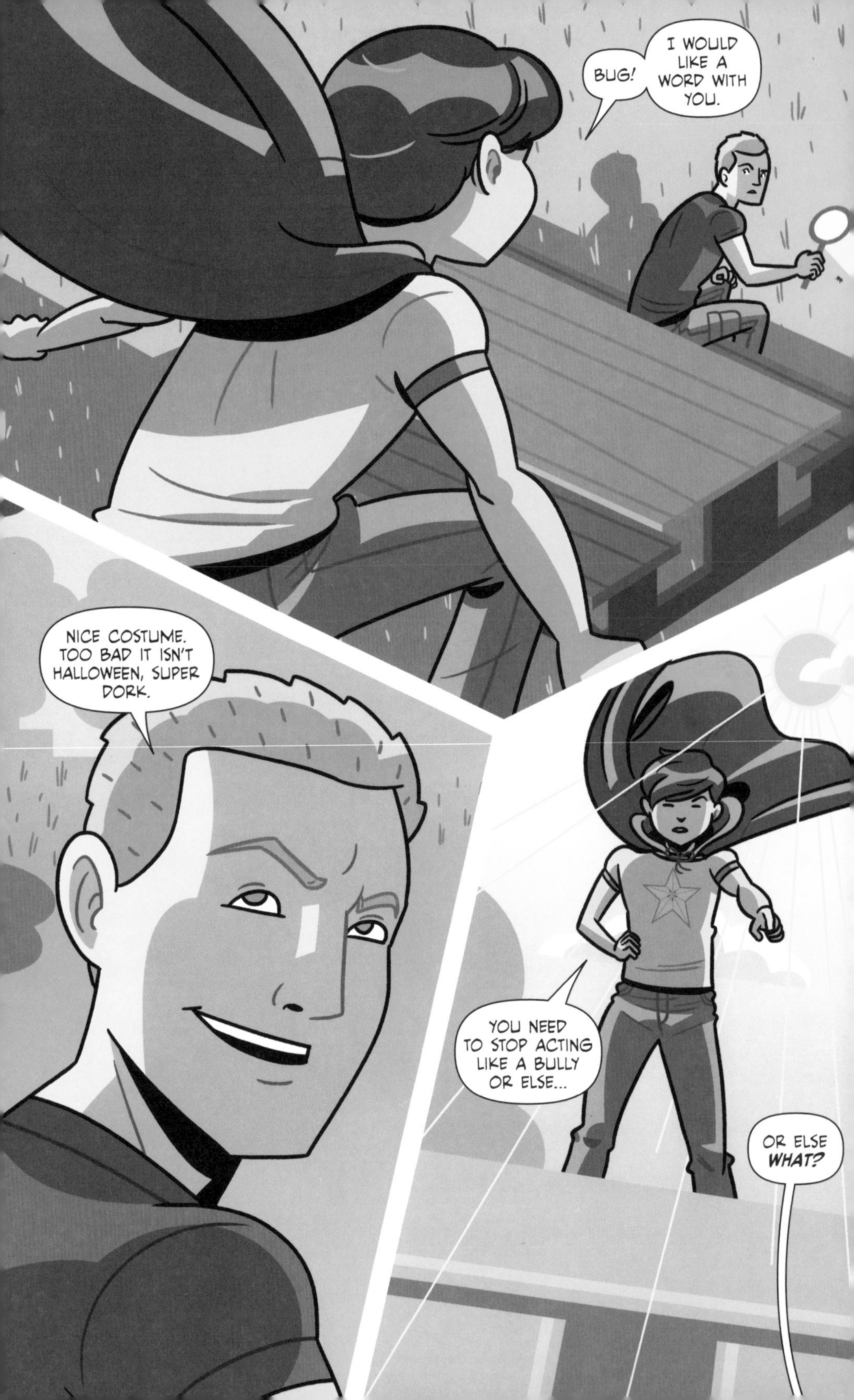
BUG!
I WOULD LIKE A WORD WITH YOU.
NICE COSTUME. TOO BAD IT ISN'T HALLOWEEN, SUPER DORK.
YOU NEED TO STOP ACTING LIKE A BULLY OR ELSE...
OR ELSE *WHAT?*

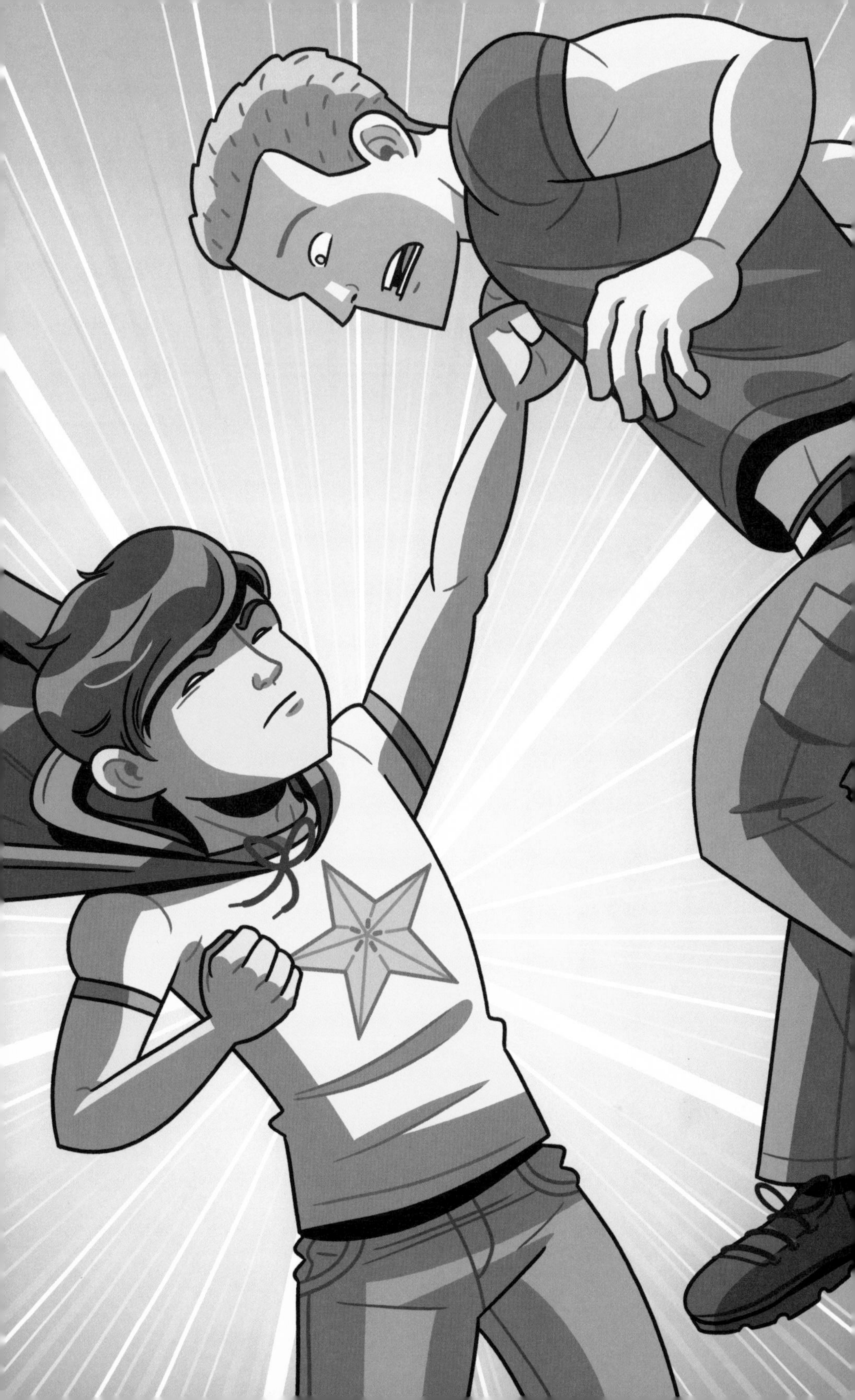

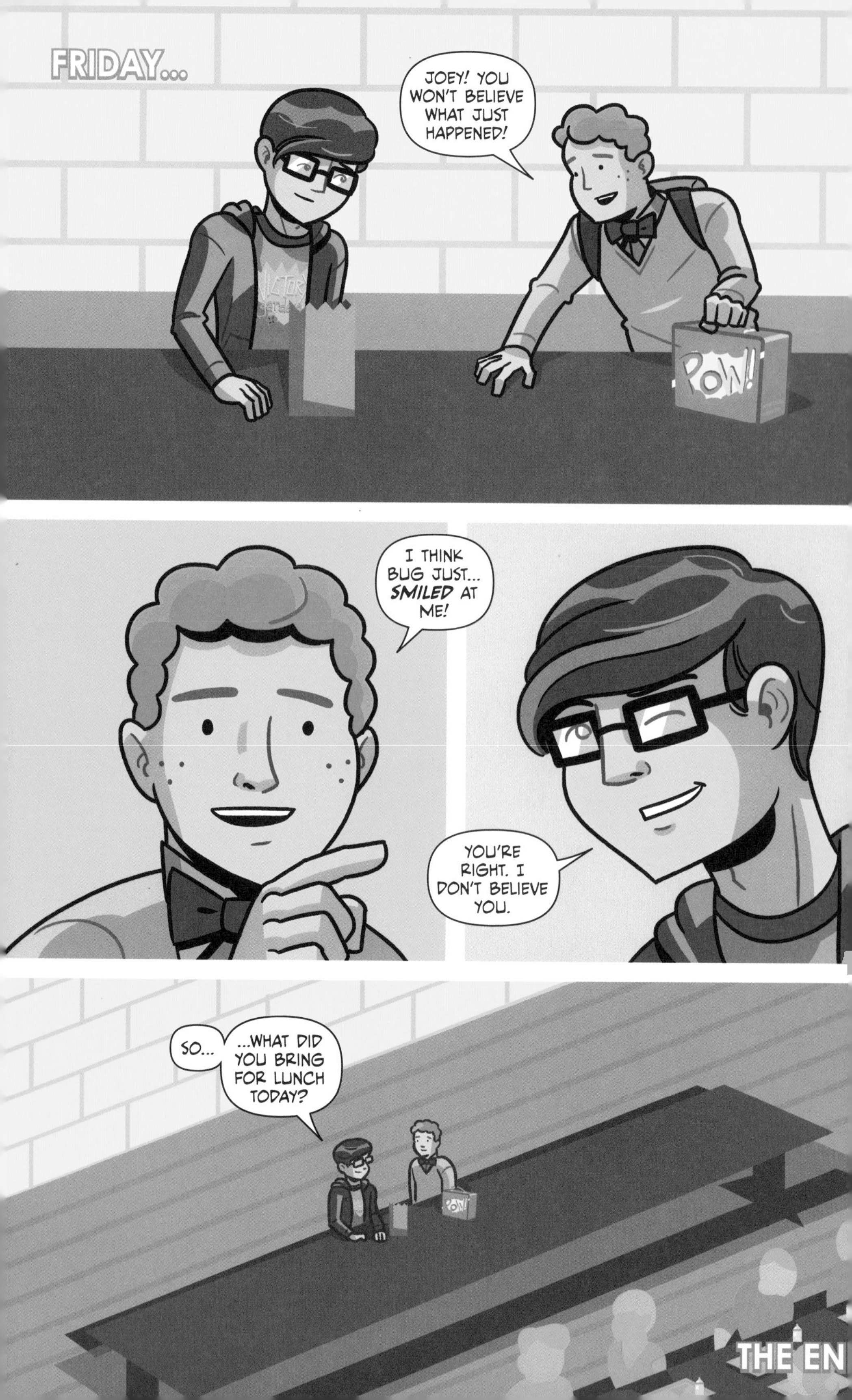
FRIDAY...
JOEY! YOU WON'T BELIEVE WHAT JUST HAPPENED!
POW!
I THINK BUG JUST... SMILED AT ME!
YOU'RE RIGHT. I DON'T BELIEVE YOU.
SO...
...WHAT DID YOU BRING FOR LUNCH TODAY?
THE EN

ABOUT THE AUTHORS

J. Torres is perhaps best known for writing the Eisner-nominated *Alison Dare* and the popular *Teen Titans Go* series, which helped earn him a Shuster Award. His graphic novels *Days Like This* and *Lola: A Ghost Story* were also listed by Young Adult Library Services Association. Upcoming projects include *Bigfoot Boy* (Kids Can Press), *Do-Gooders* (Oni Press), as well as the all-new *Josie and the Pussycats* (Archie Comics). His favorite foods are cheeseburgers, eggplant, and fried rice.

The writer would like to dedicate this book to his nephew, Majik, for not letting the bullies get the best of him.

www.jtorresonline.com

Dean Trippe is the creator of *Butterfly*, a superhero parody webcomic, co-founder and co-editor of *Project: Rooftop*, the popular superhero redesign art blog, and a contributor to *Comic Book Tattoo*, the Eisner and Harvey award-winning anthology. Dean is a lifelong superhero fan and former comic shop manager who holds an actual degree in comic books. His favorite foods are hamburgers, sweet potato fries, and carrot cake.

The artist would like to dedicate this book to his son, Emmett, whose superpower is making every day awesome and fun.

He also wishes to very much thank his great friend, Jordan Gibson, for his help with the color flats for this book; as well as his incredible wife, Sonrisa Trippe, for her advice, encouragement, and inspiration.

www.deantrippe.com

MORE COMIC BOOKS FOR EARLY READERS!

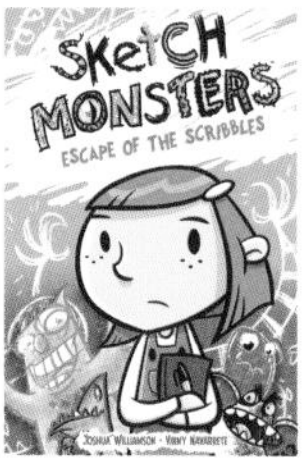
SKETCH MONSTERS
ESCAPE OF THE SCRIBBLES

SKETCH MONSTERS - VOLUME 1: ESCAPE OF THE SCRIBBLES

By Joshua Williamson & Vicente Navarette

48 pages • Color

$12.99 US • ISBN 978-1-934964-69-9

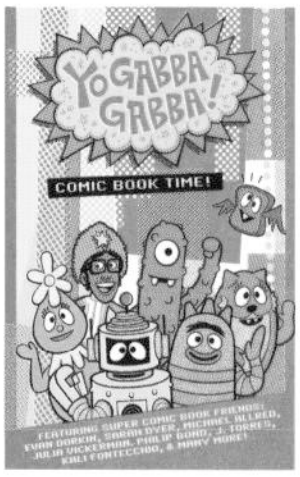
YO GABBA GABBA!
COMIC BOOK TIME!

YO GABBA GABBA! COMIC BOOK TIME! VOLUME 1

By Evan Dorkin, Sarah Dyer, Michael Allred, Julia Vickerman, Philip Bond, J. Torres, Kali Fontecchio, and more!

128 pages • Hardcover • Color

$24.99 US • ISBN 978-1-934964-49-1

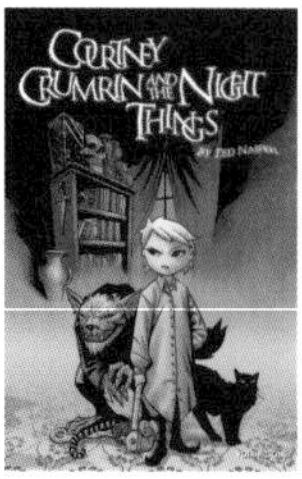
COURTNEY CRUMRIN AND THE NIGHT THINGS

COURTNEY CRUMRIN - VOLUME 1: THE NIGHT THINGS

By Ted Naifeh

128 pages • Digest • Black and White

$11.95 US • ISBN 978-1-929998-60-9

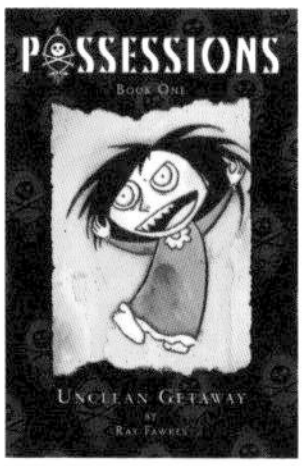
POSSESSIONS
BOOK ONE
UNCLEAN GETAWAY

POSSESSIONS - VOLUME 1: UNCLEAN GETAWAY

By Ray Fawkes

88 pages • Digest • Black, Green, and White

$5.99 US • ISBN 978-1-934964-36-1

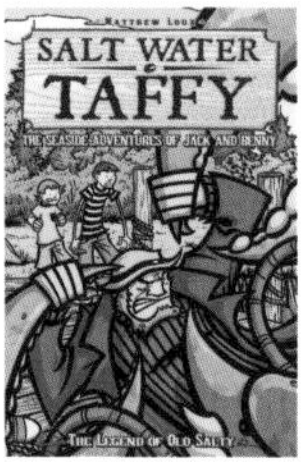
SALT WATER TAFFY

SALT WATER TAFFY - VOLUME 1: THE LEGEND OF OLD SALTY

By Matthew Loux

96 pages • Digest • Black and White

$5.95 US • ISBN 978-1-932664-94-2

For more information on these and other fine Oni Press comic books and graphic novels, visit www.onipress.com. To find a comic specialty store in your area, call 1-888-COMICBOOK or visit www.comicshops.us.

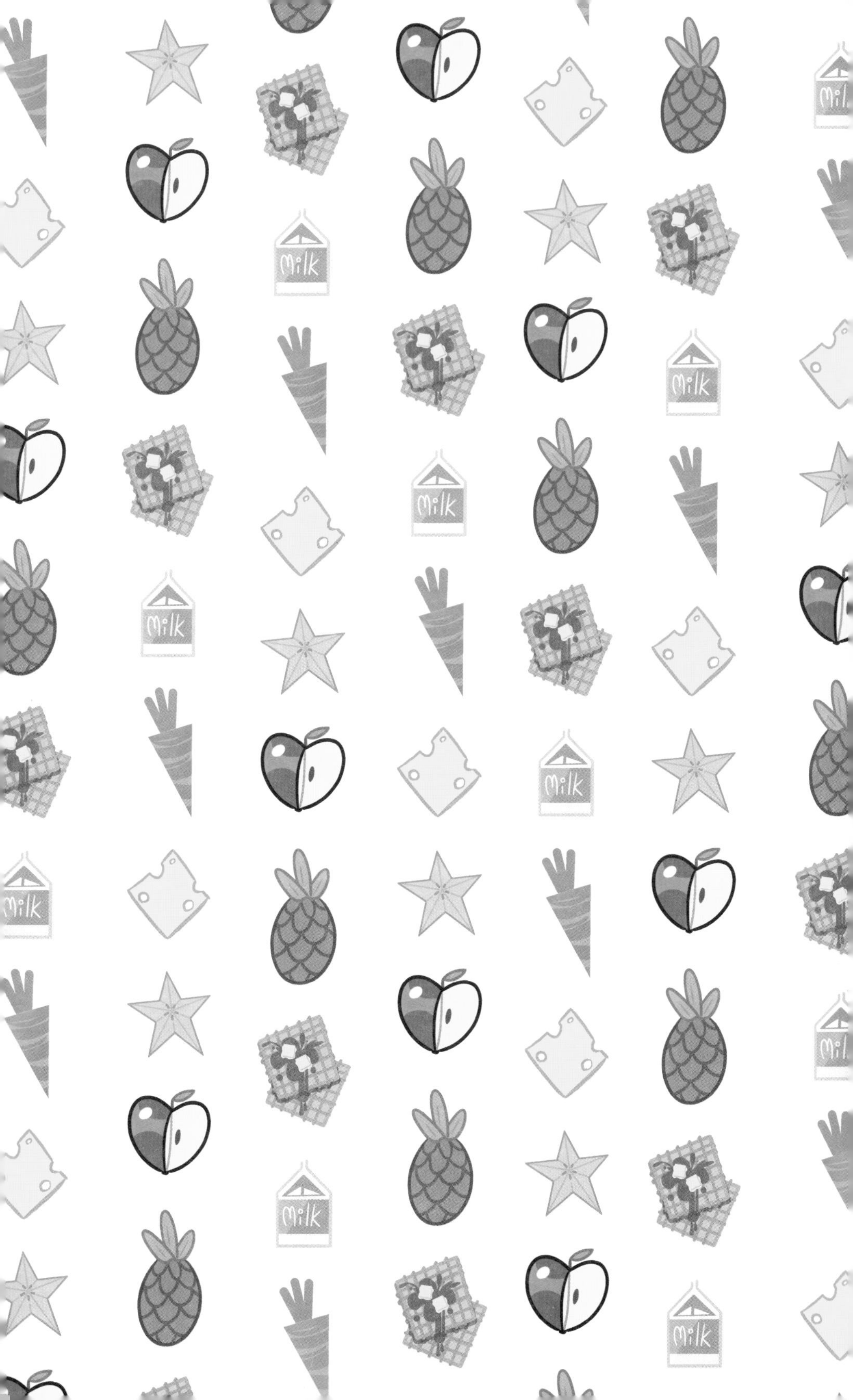
Milk

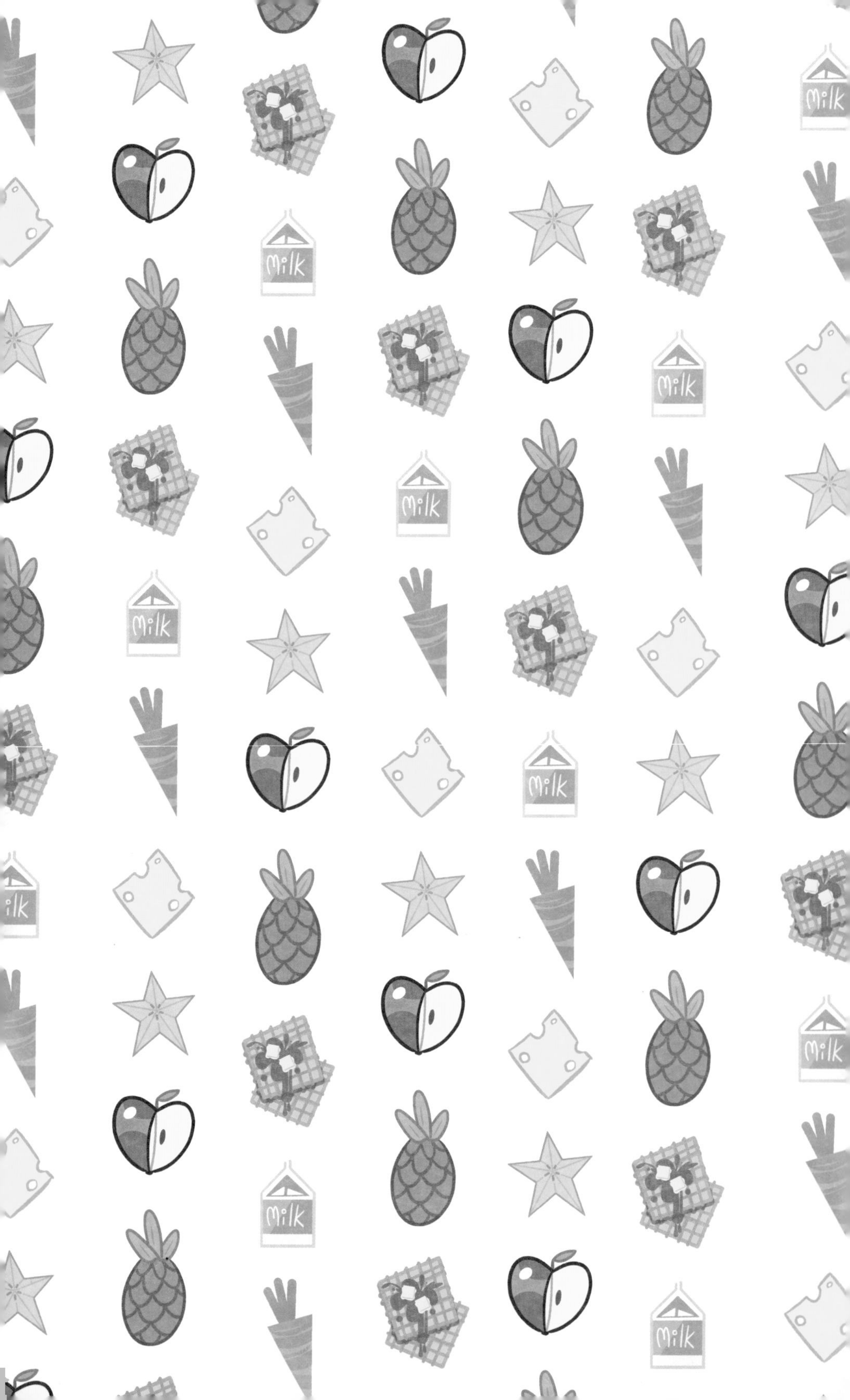
Milk